In the distant future there are only three habitable planets, Laasp, Yerak, and Isal. All the rest are covered by ice because nearby stars have cooled off or gone supernova. Only two spacecrafts, both on Laasp, are designed to travel in deep space. Both vessels must leave this planet soon. If they don't gamma rays are going to kill both ships' crew.

Starship Fane
Copyright © 2020 Thadd Evans
ISBN: 978-1-4874-3052-8
Cover art by Martine Jardin

Published by eXtasy Books Inc or
Devine Destinies, an imprint of eXtasy Books Inc

Look for us online at:
www.eXtasybooks.com or www.devinedestinies.com

STARSHIP FANE

BY

THADD EVANS

DEDICATION

Rene Magritte

CHAPTER ONE

I sat with my adrenaline pumping, worried about the future. In the last several hundred years, many stars had cooled off. At the same time, the surface temperature of nearby planets had dropped below zero. As a result, trillions of humans, Aito, and members of other races had perished. Although scientists on these planets had told millions of leaders to build galactic vessels, ones that would transport residents to warmer planets, only about eight thousand leaders paid attention.

Without warning, my contact lenses beeped, indicating that somebody was calling me. Dr. Hume, the head of a team of scientists named the National Association of Astronomers — NAA — appeared in them. He was frowning.

"Captain Adam Fiirs, you have a new assignment. You will be the pilot of the new Starship Fane, a craft that will leave soon. Three members of the NAA team liked your resume because you along with your crew landed the spacecraft Leenad on the Wen Et space station without any problems, the only pilot who has ever done that."

"Thank you, sir."

"At any rate, NAA astronomers have recently spotted two habitable planets, Yerak and Isal. Unfortunately both are light years away, so far from us that it's impossible to determine what specific life forms are on them.

"The Lergo, a new starship with two thousand passengers, will leave tonight bound for Yerak. Yours, the Fane, a much smaller craft, will leave not long after Lergo departs." He paused.

I nodded, sweating. According to a recent newspaper headline, gamma rays would strike our planet Laasp in the near future, slaughtering billions of people on all three of its continents, Yerr, Laz, and Toha along with both of its largest islands, Fot and Ry. "Talk to as many potential crew as possible. Tell us if you think they're qualified. Since there isn't much time and HR staff are busy, a PSR will pick the rest."

My mind sped up, trying to anticipate how many problems would pop up before Fane left. Would personnel selection robots—PSR—pick the best employees?

Hume stood, glowering. "If you have any questions, contact me. I have to attend a meeting with President Gravin in a few minutes."

I offered a forced grin while he rushed off. Text along with a 3D hologram of Eaaga, her co-pilot, and an Aito woman with blue skin appeared in my lenses. According to the text, when Eaaga was a teenager, she discovered math on a website. In three months she used differential calculus to design two types of shaping-shifting shuttles. She received straight A's in high school.

She attended Moro University, where she received a Bachelor's degree in science as a math major, a Master's degree in science specializing in math, and a doctorate in space vector analysis.

Several months after graduating, Intra Corporation hired her and she—along with her co-pilot—began operating the Gull, an eighty-foot-long spacecraft that transported spectrometers, food and medical supplies to and from Barmo, Zaol, and Lyen—Laasp's three moons. They did this for five years. Four months after reaching Zaol, Eaaga figured out how to use nonlinear equations along with four software applications to create better routes between all three moons.

I sent her an email, telling this potential colleague my

desire to interview her in person for this job. A 3D hologram of her came out of the background. "I'm ready. Come right over."

I entered the Gull's cockpit. It took off. Eaaga sat in front of me, her brow tight in concentration. She shoved her hand through a holographic screen.

I sat. "Have you read all of the job's requirements?"

She glared at me. "Of course. I feel that I'm more qualified for this position than anybody else."

I looked out the window while the ship zoomed over a twenty-thousand-foot- high mountain. As my adrenaline pumped, the craft went between two galactic personnel trans-porters, decelerated and docked on a planetary equipment carrier. "How many types of spacecraft have you piloted?"

"Eight. I just sent videos about this to you," she blurted.

In my lenses, the Sorm, a fifty-foot-long reconnaissance vessel, resembling a bullet, flew into a moon's crater and landed.

I blinked, impressed. "Excellent. You're hired."

"What's next?"

"My assistant will send you an email regarding that question in a few minutes." As I departed, the resumé of a potential crewmate named, Reoda, scrolled through my lenses. She was a female human with a Bachelor's degree in galactic map-making, a Master's in data analysis and a doctorate in astro-physics. Reoda was a navigator on eight galactic freighters that transported medical equipment and other goods to and from Barmo, Zaol, and Iyen.

The personnel carrier, Yoon, docked inside Space Station Glaan's largest hangar. I climbed out, walked to a cafe and sat at a table.

Reoda glowered from the opposite side of the table.

"You're late."

I winced. "Sorry. There was a lot of traffic."

"That's a lousy excuse."

I shook my head, irritated.

"According to my records, Fane hasn't been thoroughly tested in deep space. Is that correct?"

I leaned back, put off by her lousy attitude. "That is correct."

She banged her fist on the table. "As far as I'm concerned, this is a suicide mission."

I bit my lip, frustrated.

She glared at me. "Is there another ship available? One that has been field tested more thoroughly?"

"No."

"Then forget about it. Find somebody else." She rose and stomped off.

My mind sped up, trying to figure out what I would do if the other potential candidates rejected my offer.

Then a 3D hologram of Duane Goam along with his resume scrolled through my lenses. He was a Qio humanoid with purple skin. Goam graduated from Lowan High School at the top of his class. He attended Karn University in the Sen Republic, a country in Toha. He received a Bachelor's of Arts in mechanical engineering, a Master's of Arts in object programming, along with a doctorate in fusion engine statistics. Days after graduating, he moved to Laz, and started working for Membo, a company that built and repaired galactic motors and engines designed for spacecraft.

I paused, impressed, then sent him an email, asking him if he wanted to be interviewed. Seconds after, I had an incoming call and saw his blurred face before my lens could focus. He scowled at me. "We can meet in forty minutes. However, I haven't studied the job requirements. I'll look at them in a few seconds."

I entered a hangar near the top of Space Station Nas and walked toward a twenty-foot-long fusion engine. In the near distance, Goam climbed out of a twenty-foot-high routine maintenance robot — RMR — an android used to repair and update fusion engines. Nanites rose from the floor and fused together, creating a quiet room, where both of us could talk. We strolled through its liquid-like wall and sat at a table.

"Does the job interest you?" I asked.

He raised an eyebrow. "Although Fane needs more field testing, we have to leave Laasp soon. I don't look forward to the journey. But that's just the way it is. Yes, I'm interested. Will you contact me regarding the next step soon?"

"My assistant will send you an email regarding that question in a few seconds."

Goam sighed. "That is acceptable."

As I was leaving Goam, Dr. Mary Browna's curriculum vitae along with her 3D holographic ID materialized. This human had received a Bachelor's and Master's in physiology from Leam College, a school located in the United Provinces of Yerr. She was a primary care physician, who had received her medical degree from Ossen University in the Maas Republic, in Yerr. She graduated third in her class.

Noem, a hospital in Maas' capital, Ima, hired her several days after graduating. She studied the after-effects of primary cosmic rays on humans, Qio, and Aito humanoids for eight years, wanting to find out if their immune systems could be enhanced to the point where the rays wouldn't kill them. On some occasions she used alginate to place cells in the body, a technique that cured melanoma, leukemia, and other diseases.

During this time she programmed and used MEC, medical care androids, robots that helped her treat more patients. Eight years ago, she was transferred to Kab, a hospital that was understaffed.

The Yoon shuttle touched down on Secm, a transportation hub on Zaol. Its hatch opened. I left the Yoon, rushed across a platform, entered a maglev train, and sat. It sped up, zoomed through a liquid-like wall and went over Zaol's barren surface, bound for a huge crater.

Within minutes, it went over the crater's rim, descended, went through a door made of nano robots and touched down, close to Kab. I stepped off the train, walked through an entrance, then sat. Nanites came out of the floor, creating a room, a table and another chair.

Dr. Browna darted inside and plopped down. She blurted, "Sorry I'm late. The operation lasted much longer than my computer model indicated."

My stomach muscles tightened, a frustrated response. "I understand."

She glowered. "Why didn't you contact me via 3D holographic messaging?"

"I prefer face to face meetings."

This potential colleague paused, an irritated expression on her face.

"Did you get a chance to look over the job's guidelines?"

She sighed. "A little. However, judging by the mess we're in, it's the best option available. I don't want to die in a gamma burst. When do we leave Laasp?"

I repeated my instructions.

She exhaled with a tired expression on her face. "See you soon." I departed. Dr. Len Croll's resume and 3D holographic ID scrolled through my lenses. He, a Qio, received a Bachelor's and a Master's in Astrophysics from Raem, a college in Great Ra, a country in Fot. This talented student graduated with honors. He received a doctorate in Astronomy from

Paoll, a university in Great Ra.

Two days after graduating, Xea Incorporated hired him. For the next three years, he operated multiple capability radio and optical interferometric telescopes — MCIT — equipment that used the entire sound spectrum along with infrared, visible, and ultraviolet refracted light to map six planets. During this time, he along with his team of mapmaking robots used spectrometers and laser Doppler scanners to examine strange attractors along with hydrogen, oxygen, helium, and other gas ratios in all six planets' atmospheres.

I sent him an email. When his 3D holographic response appeared, I could see his jaw muscles tightened. "I'm on Iyen, charting four red giant stars. Your email regarding a job on the Fane was intriguing."

"I would like to interview you face-to-face, but you're a long way from here."

He clenched his teeth. "Interview me right now. I'm too busy to leave this area."

I bit my lip, irritated that we couldn't talk about this in person. "If you wish. Does the job interest you?"

He sighed. "Although I want to stay on Iyen, it's important to be practical. In other words, if I don't join your crew, I'll die."

I nodded.

"When and where do I go?"

I repeated my instructions.

He grimaced. "See you soon." The hologram vanished. I sent an email to Dr. Hae Lana, an Aito humanoid with turquoise skin, a woman who spoke five languages. Her response scrolled through my lenses a few seconds later. According to her resumé, she received a Bachelor's degree in three languages — English, Aito, and Qio — from Wen College in Bema, a country in Fot. She also attended Hart University in Noma, a country in Laz. After attending Hart for three years, she earned a Master's in physics. In her thesis, she wrote about the gravitational pull inside twenty different spacecraft. She received a doctorate for computer science from Hart. For her dissertation she wrote Langco, software that analyzed the differences and similarities between three languages — English, Aito, and Do Ga.

After I read through her resume, she called me. Her face, another response, came out of my lenses' background. She offered me a brief smile. "I'm aboard the shuttlecraft Yean, preparing to teach a class. I glanced over your email, thought it was worth examining. Can you meet me in three hours?"

"Yes."

"Good, see you then."

The Cenr left Secm, then sped up, veered starboard, and went around a six-foot-diameter asteroid.

The pilot's voice came out of my microscopic earplugs, "It's going to be a rough ride. Eighteen asteroids are in the way. Hold on."

I flinched. Without warning, the Cenr swerved port, then dropped and went under one of the rocky bodies.

On my left, a passenger blurted, "This is horrible. Last week somebody told me a shuttle named the Qes smashed into an asteroid."

Shivers ran up my spine. "That's too bad."

"Tell me about it. Everybody died."

I winced. The Cenr lurched starboard, then went around another one.

It docked on the Yean, half a mile from space debris. I rushed out of the Cenr, then sat in a hall. Nanites came out of the floor and formed a small room along with a table and chair. Hae Lana darted in and sat, her shoulders drooped. She exhaled, fatigue written all over her face. "That was a tough class. My students asked a lot of difficult questions."

I blinked, surprised that she, a professional, struggled with inquiries regarding language. "Are you ready for a job interview?"

"Absolutely. I glanced over the requirements. Although they're demanding, it's time for me to leave this area. Most of my colleagues know they'll be dead soon, wish they could board a starship that is headed for a safer planet or moon."

I nodded.

"What should I do next?"

I repeated my instructions.

She winced. I departed and sent Dr. Mark Doland an email. His responded with a resume and his 3D holographic ID. Dr. Doland was a human, who received a Bachelor's in entomology and a Master's in Ecology from Ulo University, a school near the middle of Graag, a country in Toha. He was an honor student and received a doctorate in botany from Nona college in Aben, a country in Fot.

When he was at Nona, this potential colleague examined the relationship between quantum mechanics and photosynthesis for three years. As a result, he learned how to create fuel for intergalactic space vessels — IC's. Two days after graduating, Parse Inc. hired him. Five months later, he shared this data with his co-worker, a biochemist, who created better prescription drugs, medicine that saved eight million lives.

I blinked, amazed by Doland's skills.

Cenar's engines roared to life. Inside its entrance, a stewardess announced, "Hurry, we'll leave soon."

I rushed inside and sat. The ship took off and flew between three other spacecraft. To my right, a female passenger said, "Thousands of travelers are hoping to reach caves, areas where they'll be safe when the gamma rays strike. With any luck they'll get there and survive."

I nodded, then glanced at her, a beautiful Qio woman. Her hands kept trembling.

"Which cave are you bound for?" she asked.

"I'm headed for a starship."

"Starships will be destroyed by the gamma ray. At any rate, good luck."

I cringed. "Which cave are you headed for?"

Her brow tightened. "Eop. It's huge, secure. It's crowded, but there is enough room for everybody."

In my mind's eye, I pictured a horrible possibility, Eop's occupants argued about the cramped space and lack of privacy.

Cenar touched down. I exited, then stepped inside a shuttle. It rose and accelerated. On my right, the driver, a metallic azure humanoid transport persons robot—TRP—said, "You're late."

"Sorry. Traffic was heavy."

The shuttle went around three flying buses, whizzed past thousand feet high skyscrapers, and zoomed over stadiums. Above us a thousand airborne cars blocked our way. The shuttle dropped, flew under them, raced between towers, went over a crowded bridge, one where thousands of people were racing in many directions.

I blurted, "Many residents are panicking."

The TRP said, "That is accurate."

To our right, an airborne truck accelerated, smashed into the front of the shuttle, and both vehicles stopped. I shuddered.

The TRP glanced at me, remarked, "Are you injured?"

"No. Just shook up."

The airborne truck operator jumped out of his vehicle, then shouted, "You're a fuckin' lousy driver." He raced toward the front of our shuttle. The TRP stepped out of it. "Sir, you ran the red light."

The operator shouted, "I'm gonna punch your lights out." He raised his fists, then swung at the robot. The TRP stepped aside. The operator stumbled, jumped up, and spun around. Then he lunged at the TRP. The robot dodged to the right. The operator's fist struck empty air, missing the android's chin. Tear gas came out of the TRP's cheek, engulfing the operator and making him cough.

The TRP turned, jumped inside the shuttle and drove off.

I winced, then glanced at the android. "You have quick reflexes."

"Thank you. I'm programmed to deal with unforeseen circumstances."

The shuttle flew over a huge crowd, shouting, "The end is near!" Soon our vehicle touched down, close to Fane. I hopped out, darted toward it and entered.

I sat in the pilot's seat. To my right, in the co-pilot's chair, Eaaga shook her head. "Captain, the gamma ray burst will arrive in three minutes."

I felt my body go cold. "Understood. Call me Adam." I waved my hand over a motion sensitive screen. The ship's engine roared louder. Within seconds, Fane shot upward.

The back of Eaaga's head jerked backward an inch, and stopped, held in place by a force field. Her seat began shaking. She blurted, "This is the fastest craft I've ever been on."

"I know the feeling."

She coughed. "At our present rate, the gamma ray burst will destroy our vessel in eighty seconds. The burst just obliterated the Lergo."

I blenched. "The wormhole will open soon."

Eaaga sighed. "I'll believe that when I see it."

CHAPTER TWO

I exhaled, trying to relax.
"It will destroy Fane in four seconds."
The wormhole materialized. Our ship entered and accelerated toward it.
"Fane is shaking so much that it will break apart in thirty seconds," my co-pilot huffed.
I clenched my teeth. Our craft left the wormhole, decelerated, and stopped shaking. I exhaled, trying to calm down. "Any problems with the hull, the crew, engines, or computer servers?"
Eaaga grimaced. "Not so far."
"Goam, any problems?"
His tense face appeared in my lenses. "No, captain."
"Call me Adam," I told Goam. "I'm tired of formal titles."
Goam blinked. "Yes, sir."
His face vanished and was replaced by Croll, the ship's Chief Galactic Mapmaker.
"Adam, we'll reach Yerak in two days," he winced. "According to my latest probe, both of its continents are ninety-eight percent jungle. We'll have to land there because nutrition staff didn't give us enough food."
I cringed at his last words. "How long will the foods last?"
He glowered as he looked over our stockpile. "A week."
My stomach muscles tightened. "Why didn't they give us more?"
"They didn't have enough time."
I bit my lip, shocked at her predicament.

Eaaga moaned. "Complications. We're in big trouble."
I squirmed. "Maybe."
She glowered at me but didn't say anything.

CHAPTER THREE

The following morning a life-size 3D hologram of M4 — a shape-shifting android that resembled a blonde human woman — appeared next to a nearby control panel. The hologram's accompanying text indicated that a new prototype of M4, manufactured by Biot Labs, would help us if we needed technical assistance.

M4's information vanished and was replaced by Security Officer Diane Fesa's resumé along with her 3D holographic ID. When she was in high school Fesa studied forensic software. She received a Bachelor's in police science, and a Master's in surveillance. She was a lieutenant in the United Provinces Army and fought in the Coastal War, a battle that lasted three years. Fesa received three gold stars for valor after the war.

Fane descended, then zoomed over towering kapoks. Weon was a jungle in one of Yerak's continents. I cringed at the sight. "This rainforest is huge, over six million square miles."

Eaaga winced. "It's the biggest I've ever seen. There is an open space forty miles from here, a spot that is close to wild legumes."

"That's a long way from our current location. Is there anything closer?"

She glared at me. "Not according to my maps."

I rubbed my chin, disappointed.

We touched down between strangler figs. Fane's disk-shaped hull separated into eleven domes. Soon all of them arranged themselves in a circle, a settlement I called Unity.

Doland's tense face materialized in our lenses. "This area is filled with nutritious legumes, enough to last us three months or longer. However, we should bring them aboard fast."

"Why fast?" I blurted.

Doland blenched. "Because Weon is filled with huge spiders."

I cringed. "How big are they?"

"Three feet or longer."

My mind sped up, trying to figure out how we would deal with them. "How many are there?"

Doland glowered. "Thousands, maybe millions. I'm still counting."

"Are they lethal?" Eaaga spat out.

Doland sighed. "M-Four is scanning the area, will have more information regarding that question soon.

"Also, I noticed one small batch of legumes nearby. There is another huge batch along with coconut trees, a mile north of our current location."

I exclaimed, "How many legumes are in the nearby batch?"

Doland scowled. "About four hundred."

Eaaga remarked, "How big are they?"

"Six inches long."

I bit my lip, terrified. "Dr. Browna, Dr. Croll, Dr. Hae Lana and Dr. Doland, collect legumes in the adjacent area immediately. The rest of you will accompany me during another journey. M-Four, can you turn into an APUT and transport us to the other legumes?" A week ago, she told me she was working on this new vehicle, an all-purpose transporter that flew over land, about six feet above it.

"Not yet. Its engines are flawed. My internal nano robots

need to repair eight bio-circuits and five bio-logic boards."

I frowned. "Does anybody have questions regarding our journey?"

M4 replied in monotone. "Not at this point in time."

The entire crew left the Fane on foot.

"Is the surrounding perimeter safe?" I asked as we entered dome A, a building near the edge of Unity.

M4 replied, "I'm still evaluating it with my echo-imager. Although Fane's MCIT examined eighteen thousand plants and eighty percent of the soil within a two-hundred-yard radius of Unity and determined that this area was ninety-five percent secure, the imager must do it again because the first probe took place when we were two light years from this location."

Eaaga announced, "According to recent scans, snail like creatures on adjacent wimba trees will spray us if we come within nine yards of the mollusks."

In front of her, Rosk winced. "My molecular organizer hasn't finished analyzing its latest probes. M-Four, is the spray toxic?"

"At this point, unknown. My imager is still evaluating it."

"Let's assume that their spray is harmless," I said. Everybody left dome A.

Not far behind M4, Goam stepped over small roses. "The gravitational waves in this area are out of phase."

"Will they affect us?" I asked.

"Undetermined. We need to know more," Goam replied.

"Let's go."

Goam offered a thumps up and we hiked forward.

Within minutes, after tramping through dense jungle, I noticed a six-foot-tall, dimly lit humanoid stranger standing ninety yards in front of us. I pointed at the entity. "Can anybody else see the alien?"

"No, they're hidden in shadows," replied M4.

Without warning, the being did an about face and darted behind a kapok. I blenched, worried. "Why did the alien leave?"

"At this point in time, unknown."

"According to my scanner, the stranger is gone, vanished into thin air."

"I'm getting the same readings," M4 said, looking at her scanner. "This has never happened to me before. There must be an explanation. I'll examine my MAW's databases."

Goam paused. "This is unsettling."

"I don't like it either," I told him. A multispectrum light and audio wave compiler — MAW — sprayed electrons. At the same time, it sent out ultrasonic beeps. When both returned to this device, a tool with maximum range of two hundred yards, it analyzed and structured the results, photos, 3D holograms, videos with soundtracks, recordings and molecular scans. When necessary MAW created graphs, ones indicating the presence and the amount of lethal airborne bacteria, deadly viruses, and contaminated water. Eighty percent of the time it took fifteen seconds to come up with helpful results.

Ahead, Rosk scowled. "Although I hear a faint scratching, I can't tell what's making the noise." He walked between dangling vines.

"My MAW is analyzing the noise," M4 said.

As I watched in horror, a three-foot-long spider jumped out from behind the vines, then bit Rosk's head off. As his body toppled over, the predator darted between ferns, plants beyond the vines, then vanished, hidden in shadows.

My body went cold with shock. I squeezed the trigger. My pistol's beam hit dirt, far from the target.

A laser beam came out of M4's wrist, then struck the

ground. "I missed the arachnid."

Eaaga's rapid-fire laser pistol clicked. "This RFL fucked up. What is wrong with it?"

Goam announced, "The spider escaped before my RFL could detect it."

Ninety percent of the time, microscopic RFL's, rapid fire laser weapons that were attached to your knuckles, could detect an attacker's body shape and hit it the first time.

Eaaga scowled. "That creature is sophisticated. It avoided your RFL's sensor."

Goam cringed. "That is correct."

I winced. "Let's take Rosk's body back to Unity and give him a proper burial."

Eaaga glowered at us. "Shouldn't we chase the creature?"

"You heard Adam. Let's go," Goam snapped.

Eaaga's brow tensed. "If you say so. But finding it again will be tough. And if we don't kill it the creature might attack Unity."

I flinched, terrified that Eaaga was correct. "Turn off your RFL's safety switch. Fire at will."

M4 commented in a monotone, "My computer model indicates that Adam's plan is a good idea."

Goam scowled. "My RFL's screen is filled with random numbers and chaotic graphs. Something is distorting the RFL's sensor."

"Shit. The same thing is happening to mine," Eaaga blurted. "This hasn't occurred before. RFL's are supposed to be sturdy."

My stomach muscles tensed. "Pay close attention to your surroundings."

Goam clenched his teeth but didn't say anything.

The next morning, when Rosk's burial ceremony was over, I organized a search party to find the spider.

Within half an hour, after our group—comprised of M4, Eaaga, Goam, Fesa and I—hiked through dense jungle, we reached a clearing. In it, haze spread and partly obscured a nine-story cylinder, a structure without any windows.

Goam glared at his wrist. "My RFL's sensor couldn't detect this building three seconds ago. This is the first time that it wouldn't notice any building. I can't figure out why the sensor failed."

Eaaga clenched her teeth. "Mine couldn't detect it either. M-Four, what do you think?"

She replied, a blank expression on her face. "There could be thousands of reasons. My MAW is organizing data. According to my MAW, something destroyed the electrons and obliterated the beeps. As a result, my MAW has created inaccurate graphs, blurred photos and hazy, useless three D holograms."

Eaaga shook her head. "Will it provide any helpful answers soon?"

"At this point, unknown."

"Let's go inside the building," I said.

Goam scowled. "Is that a good idea?"

"Maybe not. However, we need to know who or what is stopping our attempts to figure out what is inside."

"Going inside is a bad idea," he blurted.

"That's an order," I firmly stated.

Goam scowled at me but turned to face the building. "Yes sir."

Fesa frowned. "My RFL's screen is filled with random algorithms, useless results."

Then a door slid open.

Fesa glowered, looking at it. "Why did that open? It bothers me."

"We need information," I told the group. "Go inside." Our

group entered and went down a curved hall, an area with blank walls.

"My RFL's screen is filled with random dots, can't provide any answers. I hate it," Eaaga announced

"My MAW isn't any help either," M4 said.

My stomach muscles tightened. "Keep probing." Soon the hall became darker. Within seconds, I reached out. "The wall is gone."

"Adam, you're correct," Eaaga blurted.

We walked. To our right and left, boulders blocked our way. All of us kept going and stopped at the edge of a dimly lit canyon.

Goam broke the silence, "Somebody or something has transported us to another spot. I can't figure out why. M-Four, any thoughts?"

"Not enough data to provide any helpful answers." She pointed to the right. "Lets cross that ledge."

Everybody continued on, following her advice.

CHAPTER FOUR

We reached a cave and entered. We came upon stairs that curved to the right, around an empty space and climbed it. To our left, there was a blank wall. Ahead, the steps jerked to the left, several inches.

Eaaga pointed at them. "They're moving. That's odd."

"Yes, odd," Fesa agreed.

They stopped in front of a dark entrance.

"Why did the steps stop appearing in front of an entrance that is poorly lit? I don't like it," Eaaga wondered.

I urged her on. "Keep going." To our left, fifty feet from the entrance that was directly in front of us, another stairway popped out of the wall, went straight across the room and stopped at another wall, a location that was to the right of the one that was in front of us. At that location, a poorly illuminated entry opened. To the left of the entrance that was directly in front of us, a catwalk came out of the wall, and went by our group. I glanced over my shoulder. Behind us, the catwalk stopped on the opposite wall. In front of the catwalk a door opened.

Fesa winced. "What is going on? Adam, which entrance should we take? All the rooms they lead to are dark. I can't see what it's inside them."

Eaaga frowned. "What about the room that is in front of the catwalk?

I hesitated, weighing options, then looked straight ahead. "Eaaga, hike across the catwalk and go inside that room. Fesa, Goam enter the room that is directly in front of us. M-Four, follow me. You and I are going inside the room on our right. Everybody keep in contact via your contact lenses. Let's regroup back here in fifteen minutes."

Eaaga and Fesa glared at me, while Goam's brow tightened.

M4 and I entered our room and came upon a dimly lit jungle. To our left and right, there were hundreds of thorn trees, obstacles that made it impossible to explore those areas. Ahead, there were only ferns. We pushed them aside and hiked. I flinched. "It's difficult to see anything clearly because it's dark."

"Affirmative." She glanced over her shoulder and pointed behind her. "The door has vanished."

I winced, then glanced in the direction the door had been, but only noticed towering ferns, plants with six-inch-long worms on them. "You're correct. Can you change into an APUT?"

"Not at this point in time."

I cringed, then looked straight ahead. "Let's investigate this area. There might be another entrance nearby."

"Acknowledged. However, the only objects my MAW detects are strangler fig trees, ferns, amoebas, dirt, and green worms. Do you think the door was designed to vanish the minute we entered this jungle? In other words, is it possible that anybody who enters this area triggers a software program that destroys the door?"

Chills went up my spine. "Thoughtful questions. I wish I had an answer. Unfortunately, my lenses' probes and my RFL's scan results are the same as yours."

"Agreed, it is unfortunate."

Ahead, about two hundred yards away, hidden behind hundreds of poorly lit strangler fig trees, a beast roared. I winced. "Can your MAW ID that creature?"

"No. For unknown reasons, that equipment is

malfunctioning, can only ID the flora and fauna that I mentioned before."

I bit my lip, frustrated. "Trouble."

"Affirmative."

"Can you update your MAW so that it works properly?"

She replied, stony faced. "I am."

My stomach muscles tightened, an annoyed response. "The others haven't contacted me via their lenses."

"They haven't contacted mine either."

I bit my lip. "We need solutions."

"Affirmative."

Both of us tramped on in ankle deep mud while the smell of rotten meat grew stronger. I said, "Although something stinks, I can't tell what it is. Can you?"

"No sir." We kept going.

Several minutes later both of us halted. Ahead in the near distance, a creature that was hidden behind palmettos snorted, brushed against them and they shook.

I flinched. "Whatever species that is, it's so huge that it pushes anything that is in its way aside."

"Affirmative."

I raised my arm, aiming my weapon in that direction. "It's coming this way."

"Affirmative."

Without warning, it moved to the left, shoving aside kapok trees. I flinched. "Is it stalking us, eating or wandering?"

"For unknown reasons, my MAW can't detect its exact size, shape or intentions."

I flinched. "Can't detect them. That's odd."

"Affirmative."

The creature stopped.

My adrenaline pumped harder. "Our bullets aren't big enough to stop it."

"According to my probability graph, you are correct."

Much to my surprise, the beast continued on, moving in the same direction, knocking lupuna trees aside. I exhaled, releasing tension. "It's leaving."

"Affirmative."

"We need to find everybody else. Unfortunately, my lenses can't locate them. Can your MAW or lenses do that?"

"They cannot."

"That's horrible. Something or somebody is destroying our equipment. When you find out, tell me who is what it is."

"Yes sir."

Normally, when these devices were in auto mode, they would call my colleagues every five minutes. Chills ran up my spine. "Let's search for those wild legumes. In the meantime update your MAW. If you're lucky it will help us find the others. After we gather enough legumes the entire crew should leave Yerak ASAP. This planet is too dangerous to stay on."

"Yes sir. I repaired some of my MAW's functionality. According to it, that huge patch of legumes is half a mile from us, due north of this location."

I blinked, surprised. "What was wrong with your MAW?"

"At this point, unknown."

I shuddered. Our wrist-mounted laser beams switched on and we started cutting our way through dense underbrush, a shadowy area that was beneath the jungle canopy.

Twenty minutes later, I said, "It's a good thing that our laser cutters are working. Otherwise both of us couldn't get this far."

"Affirmative."

Both of us came upon a small clearing. At the opposite end, a tiny monkey scampered up a palm. I pointed at the tree. "Coconuts."

"Affirmative."

Near the middle of the clearing, three shadowy figures stepped out from behind a towering bush.

I pointed at them. "Is that Goam, Fesa, and Eaaga?"

"Affirmative."

CHAPTER FIVE

We walked up to them.

"We lost track of you when you were in the tower," M4 said.

"What tower?" Goam asked, perplexed.

I blinked, startled. "The one that all of us entered." I offered more details.

Fesa glared at me. "You must be kidding."

"I am not. Where have all three of you been during the last half an hour?"

Fesa winced. "In this area. Look around, see for yourselves."

I hesitated, baffled. "Weren't all of you worried because M-Four and I vanished?"

Eaaga snapped at me. "Of course. We were searching for both of you."

Goam shook his head. "I wasn't that worried. This area is dense. It's hard to see anybody even if they're thirty feet away. However, my guess is that we would have found you soon if all of us kept looking."

M4 offered an explanation for the bizarre occurrence. "Eaaga, Fesa, Goam, a stranger altered your perception."

"I don't believe it," Eaaga spat. "Nobody altered mine."

Fesa shook her head.

Goam's brow tightened. "That is unlikely."

"The facts speak for themselves," M4 remarked, trying to convince the others. "They might have used a scanner or another type of device. Figuring out how they altered it could be difficult. "

Eaaga frowned. "There must be a rational explanation. I don't believe in any psychic voodoo shit."

"If you think of a rational explanation let me know," M4 replied

Eaaga glowered. "I don't like smart ass robots."

My jaw muscles tightened, irritated by Eaaga's comments.

I noticed Fesa's jaw muscles tighten, too. "M-Four, your comment regarding our altered perception is unusual. I've studied battle tactics for years, dealt with hundreds of camouflage techniques during black ops, and know a great deal about hundreds of online jamming procedures. Yet they weren't like this."

Goam sighed. "I have used at least eight thousand types of code, computer syntax that creates fake videos, ones that fool most people's contact lenses and MAW probes. However, that syntax doesn't function this effectively." With the answers eluding us, our group trekked on and looked for legumes.

Soon a small floating screen appeared above M4's wrist. She examined it with a blank expression on her face. "Wild legumes are close to the coconut palms."

"Let's gather legumes and coconuts ASAP. When we're finished, everybody will head for Unity," I ordered.

"Yes captain," Eaaga replied.

Everybody went to work and I turned to M4. "Can you change into an APUT and take the food to Unity?"

"Affirmative."

I told everybody else about my plan to leave Yerak ASAP.

Eaaga disagreed. "Yerak isn't that bad. Aren't you overreacting?"

My stomach muscles tensed, annoyed by her response. "We're leaving this planet ASAP."

Eaaga glared at me. Goam shrugged and Fesa frowned.

M4 returned from carrying the first load to Unity, then touched down. To our left, faraway, hidden in the jungle, we heard a scraping sound become louder.

Goam climbed down a palm, coconuts in hand. He squinted in the direction of the scraping. "I can't see what's making that noise. Can anybody else?"

M4 changed into her female human form. "I can't. My MAW probes are useless, only display meaningless dots."

"M-Four did you tell everybody at Unity about my plan to leave Yerak ASAP?"

"Affirmative."

Eaaga sighed. "Not that topic again. Yerak looks safe."

Suddenly a six-foot-long umber spider darted out from behind towering weeds.

Fesa pointed at it, her arm aimed upward. "That arachnid is coming this way. Adam, should I fire?"

My adrenaline rushed faster. "If it comes within fifteen feet of us, yes."

Eaaga aimed her hand at it, ready to spray ammo. "Its jaws are twitching. That thing is ugly."

I yelled at the creature, "Stop or we'll shoot." It advanced.

"It doesn't care," Goam blurted.

"Oh my god," Fesa called out.

Everybody discharged their weapons. Bullets and laser beams hit the creature. It squealed. *Eeeeeya.*

As chills ran down my spine in horror, the spider reached out, grabbed Fesa's head and tore it off. More ammo hit the arachnid, destroying its legs. The intruder collapsed, its thorax twitching. Bullets struck its jaws. It screeched. *Eeeeeya.* Another spider jumped out of darkness, seized Fesa's corpse, then spun around, raced into the jungle, and vanished, hidden by it.

"Horrible!" Goam snapped.

Eaaga pointed at palms. "Three more spiders are coming. Son of a bitch."

"M-Four change into an APUT and take us to Unity," I shouted.

She complied. All of us jumped on. The entire crew discharged their weapons. Within seconds, one of the creatures keeled over.

"M-Four, move faster or we're dead," Eaaga yelled.

Both spiders spit venom at us. Some of it landed on my sleeve. I cringed. "The venom is eating away the material."

"We're in a chaotic situation," Goam said.

CHAPTER SIX

Not far beyond the arachnids, to our left, six more darted out from between towering ferns.

Goam sprayed them with ammo. "Bastards." Two spiders fell over, their jaws torn to pieces. The other six scampered toward us. Laser beams killed two, slicing off their heads.

Behind them, on our right, eight more rushed out of the shadows the hair on the legs quivering.

Eaaga pointed at them. "Watch out."

Text appeared in my contact lenses. *Can't reach Dr. Browna or anybody else at Unity.* I flinched.

My ammo struck five spiders, slicing their eyes out.

"I'm not a soldier," Goam shouted.

APUT went over a twenty-foot wide stream, one with thick underbrush on both sides of its narrow shores.

"They're behind us. They've stopped at the opposite shore," Eaaga called out.

Goam sighed. "Let's hope they don't cross it."

"That makes two of us," Eaaga exclaimed.

APUT touched down near Unity. Everybody climbed off and M4 reverted into her prior form.

Doland walked up to us, his lips trembling. "Adam, M-Four told me about your plan to leave Yerak ASAP. Have you changed your mind?"

"No."

Doland glowered. "During the last thirty minutes everybody at Unity tried contacting every member of your party with our lenses. Unfortunately, we couldn't reach any of you. The only thing we heard was static."

My mind sped up, trying to come up with the best solution as I told him about Fesa's death.

Doland winced. "Adam, are you going back to reclaim her body?"

Chills ran up my spine. "No. It's too dangerous."

Doland glared at me.

"If there is enough time, we need to find out why some of our lenses' tools have failed," I said, putting an end to our discussion about Fesa.

"There are thousands of variables to consider," M4 remarked in a monotone.

Doland sighed. "It will take time to analyze bacteria, dirt, airborne viruses, plant contents and a variety of other factors."

"He is correct. It will take a great deal of time."

Eaaga didn't want to change the subject. "Adam, we need to find Fesa's body. She needs a decent burial."

"Going back is too dangerous."

"Damn it, it's the right thing to do."

"Like I said, it's too dangerous. Help M-Four and the others. Our food needs to be organized."

Eaaga glared at me and stomped off.

Hours later, at dusk while everybody was inside a transparent dome, examining computer screens and 3D holograms, trying to determine what was jamming our devices, Hae Lana, glanced over my shoulder. Much to my surprise, she rose to her feet. "We have a visitor."

CHAPTER SEVEN

I spun around, then looked outside. In the near distance, a five-foot-tall humanoid alien with mottled skin took a few steps toward us.

"The entity doesn't have any eyes. Who or what the hell is it?" Goam blurted.

"You tell me," Browna said.

"The alien told me her name is Soaa. She is a member of the Ditu race," Hae Lana told us.

My lenses sent neutrinos into Soaa's mind. The subatomic particles didn't return. I paused, disappointed. "M-Four, my lenses' neutrinos aren't working. Can you repair the lenses' neutrino transmitter?"

"I cannot."

I bit my lip. "Why?"

"For unknown reasons, the moment we touched down on Yerak, every crew member's NT stopped sending subatomic particles into anybody's mind. It could take months to repair the NT's because I can't determine why they have broken down. According to a recent MAW diagnostic test, one possibility is that Plasmon's are interfering with the transmitter's functionality."

My jaw muscles tightened. When necessary, NT, neutrino transmitter, probes helped me along with other members of the crew understand aliens and strangers.

Dr. Browna scowled. "Hae Lana, how do you communicate with her?"

"She sends out and receives weak electrical signals, her

language. My lenses' LCS translated the response."

"Did you program it to translate them?" I asked. In Language Conversion software's default mode it deciphered 43 languages. However, an IT professional could create syntax that allowed it to translate hundreds or thousands more.

Hae Lana grinned. "Yes."

Browna remarked, "Impressive."

"Using Hae Lana's LCS as a guide I wrote a better version, then exported it in everybody's lenses. Every crew member will be able to understand Soaa's remarks in a few moments," M4 replied.

Eaaga frowned. "M-Four, that's great. However, you can't repair our lenses' NT. Is that correct?"

"Yes, that is correct."

"And you can't destroy airborne viruses or whatever it is that won't allow us to contact each other via our lenses. Is that correct?"

"That is correct."

Eaaga shook her head. "As far as I'm concerned robots make too many mistakes. Most of them should be scrapped."

My jaw muscles tightened. "Eaaga, we need constructive criticism."

She glared at me. "You need honest criticism."

Hae Lana thanked M4 for updating our lenses' LC. Then she said she was grateful that M4 had repaired our lenses' export function in the last few minutes.

The robot nodded.

Then Hae Lana informed us about the arachnids. "Soaa says that we have entered the spider's territory. The arachnids call themselves the Kicra. They plan to kill all of us."

"Shit," Eaaga burst out.

Hae Lana grimaced. "Adam, Soaa and three of her friends—Xa Om, Ze Ma, and Wo Ra—who wanted to leave Yerak immediately because more lethal flies—insects that has been in hibernation for eighty years—would wake soon. Hours after they emerge, these insects, called Repa, will fill the air in every direction. Their bite is fatal to many species."

I flinched. "Are we one of those species?"

Browna replied, "Adam, Hae Lana just exported her file regarding this topic into my lenses. Yes we are."

"We are. That's horrible."

Browna nodded.

Goam glowered. "Why don't the Kicra slaughter the Ditu?"

Hae Lana answered him. "According to Soaa, every Ditu's body is filled with neurotoxins. Years ago, a Kicra ate a Ditu. Within half an hour, the Kicra died, the result of that poisoning."

Goam scowled. "Will our spacesuits protect us?"

"According to design specifications, no," M4 informed us.

Eaaga grew frustrated. "We need to leave Yerak ASAP."

"Doland, Croll, anybody, have we gathered enough wild legumes to last for several months?" I asked, feeling everyone's growing frustration.

Doland cringed. "Enough to last for one month."

Chills ran up my spine. "According to one of my probability charts, one isn't enough. Two would be better."

Eaaga snapped, "We can't eat them if we're dead. Let's get out of here now."

"We need to think about this more," I said, trying to calm her down. "If there isn't enough food, we'll starve to death long before we land on Isal. Croll, how long will it take to reach it?"

"Based on a preliminary analysis, about three months."

My mind sped up, trying to determine if there were any problems with his estimation. "What do you mean by preliminary?"

"Although my MCIT created forty maps, many are

flawed."

I winced. "Why are they flawed?"

"Rapid acceleration and deceleration has damaged has some of MCIT's lenses, their bio-circuits, and software. Repairing them will take time."

"How much time?"

"Unknown. All eight MCIT's are new and complex. Engineers and geneticists designed their bio-circuits, equipment that is similar to the human eye. As a result the telescopes learn faster than any prior model. I've never seen anything like them before, don't know which parts are likely to break down."

"Croll, you're experienced. Doesn't that help?"

"Of course it does, Adam. However, I didn't build these MCIT's. A huge team did. I'm only one man. Checking every inch of these is a slow process. If my lenses examination software moves too fast it could miss something."

I worried about Croll's ability to understand the MCIT's capabilities and limitations.

"Adam, although Fane's laser beams and quantum computers are designed to create and use wormholes, doing so is not an exact science," Goal remarked. "Each wormhole is different. Some have stronger gravitational pull than others. We won't know for sure how long it takes to go through one until Fane enters it."

"Adam, are Soaa and her friends coming aboard?" Eaaga asked.

"Yes."

"If all of them do we'll starve to death."

"All of them are coming aboard," I said through clenched teeth.

Eaaga shook her head. "Adam, you're making a big mistake."

My stomach muscles tightened. "I'll take that chance."

In the far distance, a scraping noise became louder. A spider's mouth appeared in my mind.

Everybody but M4 said the same thing had happened to him or her in the last few seconds.

Hae Lana jumped in with her suggestion. "Adam, a second ago Soaa told me a Kicra sent that picture into your mind. It's a tool they use to confuse and scare their victims. As a result, the victims feel overwhelmed and are less likely to fight back."

"What are we waiting for?" Eaaga burst out. "If we don't leave Yerak immediately everybody will die."

"I can't see what is coming. Can anybody else?" I asked.

"No. I hate it."

I flinched at Eaaga's response. "Hae Lana, when will Soaa's friends arrive?"

Soaa looked at us. "Wha-what when? About thirty minutes from now. That's a rough guess."

I blinked, surprised that Soaa understood my question.

"Can't her friends move faster?" Eaaga wailed. "Hello, hello, everybody. If we stay here for six more minutes our chances of getting out of this place alive drop by thirty percent."

I sighed. "Eaaga, be patient."

"I don't want to die!"

In the near distance, all five fourteen-foot-long spiders scampered out of the jungle.

"A-a-Adam, bigger Kicra have arrived." Soaa hid behind me.

I flinched. "Understood."

Browna glowered. "They're just standing there. Are they going to attack?"

Soaa stammered, "G-g-going to attack? Unknown. They're speaking to each other."

Browna's lips tightened. "What are they saying?"

"The-the-they are saying that they will strike in eight seconds."

"Get ready to fight," Eaaga yelled.

"Shoot to kill," I ordered.

CHAPTER EIGHT

The spiders raced toward us, spitting. All the crew fired. One creature howled. *Zooooon.*

"Th-th-that is a cry of pain," Soaa told us.

"Die, you assholes," Eaaga shouted.

More beams and ammo struck them. Much to my surprise, they stopped, then spun around, took off and disappeared into the jungle.

Eaaga raised her fist. "We scared them away."

Soaa shook her head. "No, the-they will return."

I flinched. "When?"

Soaa aimed her palm toward me. "Wh-wh-when? Some-sometime before dawn. That's my my guess."

Browna scowled at her. "Soaa, how do you know they will return before dawn?"

"I-I kn-know because past experiences inda-indicate they will."

Eaaga sighed. "We should leave Yerak now, before they re-turn."

"According to my latest probe, in the last five seconds air-borne protozoa have shorted out some of our weapon's cir-cuits. As a result, hitting a Kicra will be more difficult," M4 informed us.

My adrenaline pumped faster. "This is an order. Put as many legumes inside the domes as you can. If you're tired, rest. If everybody is too exhausted his or her aim will be off."

Eaaga glared at me. "I can't believe we aren't leaving right now."

"Do what you are told."

"Yes captain." She hurried away.

I began thinking about the tower. Text about Soaa appeared in my lenses, the result of my wrist-mounted scanner probing her skin. Although the WMS was new, it was the only way I could find out more about her. At the age of four, like many Ditu, she started deciphering weak electrical signals, all of them given off by kapoks and sabal palmettos. Because the signals, ones that made her skin tingle, consisted of a complex combination of long and short electrical charges, it took a lot of practice to memorize and understand all of them.

With the help of her mother and father, she figured out more months later, including those coming from strangler figs, vines, wimba and Pallas trees. Her parents told Soaa it would take a long time for her to decipher signals coming from every plant and tree in the adjacent Weon jungle. In a few years, Soaa would know how to control the electrical charges her body was giving off. During this time, her body would emit odors, scents that could help her communicate with strangler figs and other trees.

It might take years, maybe a lifetime, to reach all of these goals. Every Ditu was different. When some were five years old, they started a short conversation with lupuna trees. Others, who were the same age or older, figured out how to conduct a brief one with kapoks. A handful of children could converse with vines and strangler figs for hours.

I paused, amazed by the Ditu's ability to communicate with different plant species. My microscopic WMS sent this discovery to all of my colleague's scanners.

At dusk, a crunching noise came closer and grew louder. I blinked, then looked up as three Ditu—a man, a woman and a little girl—arrived. "Welcome. What are your names?"

The man replied to me, his translated answer coming out

of my earplugs, "I am Xa Om."

Does he understand the response that my lenses offered? I couldn't tell.

The woman spoke. Her translated response came out, "My name is Ze Ma." She hugged the girl and said, "This is my daughter, Wo Ra."

"A child is coming with us?" Eaaga exclaimed behind me. "That's a bad idea."

I bit my lip. "She is coming with us. I don't want to talk about it anymore."

Eaaga glared at me. "She is going to get hurt. When she does, don't blame me."

"No one will blame you. Quit complaining. If Wo Ra has any complaints or questions, help her."

"Yes captain." She stomped away.

Browna sighed. "That didn't go well, Adam."

"Eaaga must learn to compromise. She is an outstanding co-pilot. Unfortunately, when it comes to bringing aboard new passengers, she has a lot of learn."

Browna paused, her forehead tight. "Eaaga might have a point. We don't know if they'll die from heart attacks from Fane's high speeds."

My jaw muscles tightened. "If they stay here, they'll die."

Browna flinched. "That's true." She turned to Soaa and asked, "Why do the rest of the Ditu want to remain on Yerak?"

"Wha-wha-what is Yerak?"

Browna paused again, her forehead tight from concentration. "What do you call this area?" She pointed at the surroundings.

Soaa commented, "Oloo."

Browna offered a brief smile. "Why do the rest of the Ditu want to remain in Oloo?"

"The-the-they believe that Naax, its spirit, will protect

them."

Browna winced. "And you along with your friends don't accept that?"

"I-I do not. Xa Om and Ze Ma trust me, believe that my decision to leave Oloo is a good plan. Wo Ra wants to stay close to her mother."

Browna hesitated, her eyes shifting back and forth. "Soaa, do other Ditu argue with you, point out that leaving Oloo breaks any laws?"

"Ya-ye-yes they do. Yesterday, Naen Ot, the tribal leader, told me that he and several members of the Council would come to Unity to stop the four of us from leaving Oloo."

Browna winced. "How will he stop you?"

"H-he told me that he along with other Council members will drag us away and tie us up. After your craft leaves, he and others will release us."

Doland sighed. "More complications. I need to gather more legumes." He rushed off.

Soaa touched my hand. "Y-y-your salty odor is unfamiliar."

I shrugged, not sure what to say.

"An-and it doesn't change enough, won't tell me anything else about you."

I blinked, surprised. "Do the Ditu use their body odor to speak to each other?"

"Y-ye-yes. However, using it to talk to you and your friends will be difficult because your body's fragrance doesn't respond to mine."

My mind sped up, trying to determine how to deal with this problem. I sent a question regarding this topic to other crew with my lenses. The crew didn't respond. I winced, then told them about the equipment failure.

M4 said, "I just scanned everybody's lenses. Figuring out what the problem is and repairing it will take time."

41

I flinched. "How much time?"

"Unknown."

Not long after midnight, a rustling, barely audible, grew louder.

My heart pounded. "I can't see them, but I can hear some Kicra. They have arrived in the last few seconds. For some reason, my lenses can't detect them."

Eaaga shook her head. "It's only the wind."

Yat took a few steps. "Yes. It's only the wind. Adam, you're too jumpy, hearing creatures that aren't there."

I bit my lip. The rustling, a faint sound moved away. "They have departed. Did you hear them leave?"

"No. Adam, you need to calm down. Like I said, it's only the wind blowing leaves."

"Yat is correct," Eaaga said. "Adam, you're tired, not paying attention."

"Your lenses couldn't detect them?"

Eaaga shook her head.

Yat frowned. "Not at all."

Thirty minutes later, a faint scraping, barely audible, became louder.

"The Kicra have returned," I murmured.

Eaaga smirked. "Not again. Adam, you need more sleep."

Yat paused. "The only things I hear are leaves blowing in the wind."

Eaaga chuckled. "The Kicra aren't here. They'll probably arrive at dawn, when we're half asleep."

I sipped coffee, trying to stay awake. "Aren't here? Maybe. Arrive at dawn? In other words, you assume that they will depart and come back then? We'll see."

Yat turned to the right. "Adam, there are two harmless worms on the ground. They might have been making the noise that you heard."

Eaaga yawned. "They're no threat." She yanked a legume out of her pocket and took a bite. "It tastes awful."

Without warning, four fifteen-foot-long Kicra rushed out from behind towering bushes.

"What the—," Yat exclaimed. He, Eaaga and I discharged our weapons. One creature ripped off his arm. Yat screamed, "It's . . ."

I winced as the arachnid cut his body in half with a claw.

Browna jumped out of dome B, spraying bullets.

Ammo and laser beams from her weapon along with others struck the intruders. They squealed, then spun around and rushed into the jungle.

Browna came to our aid. "It happened so fast."

Eaaga blurted, "Too fast. They took Yat's body."

My mind sped up, trying to come up with a better plan.

Soaa sprinted out of dome C. "Th-th-this is horrible."

M4 rushed out of dome E. "I would have come sooner. Unfortunately three of my bio-circuits shorted out. Repairing them took longer than my computer model predicted."

Doland sprinted out of dome F. "We'll have more legumes in a few hours. When our crew achieves that goal, everybody aboard might have to go without food for a week or longer before Fane reaches Isal. However, knowing that the Kicra are dangerous we should leave Yerak when there are enough legumes."

My stomach muscles tightened. "Understood. We'll leave then."

Croll darted out of dome G. "I woke up a few seconds ago. Heard the conversation. Leaving soon is important."

Eaaga scowled. Browna cringed.

I shouted orders. "There are too many Kicra. If we chase them, they will slaughter more crew. Everybody should remain in Unity until we leave Yerak."

Everyone else agreed.

In the late morning, when several of us were outside the domes, close to them, M4 announced, "Thirty Kicra have arrived."

Eaaga glowered. "Are you sure? I can't see or hear them."

"I'm sure. They're hiding in the nearby Weon, communicating with each other by rubbing their legs against their friend's jaws and legs."

"I don't believe you. My lenses and RFL can't detect the arachnids."

Soaa defended M4. "M-M-Four's statement is t-true."

I blenched. "Everybody, pay attention to M-Four's warning."

Doland agreed with Eaaga. "She's is probably correct. My lenses and RFL only detect moving snails and crawling ants."

"The Kicra asked the snails to block your lenses and RFL probes," M4 explained. "The mollusks are using scents and microscopic spores to do it."

Eaaga shook her head. "The snails are too stupid to do that."

M4 paused with a blank expression on her face.

Doland grinned. "Eaaga is right. I've never heard of snails doing that."

Above M4's wrist, a floating screen turned toward Eaaga and Doland. She pointed at it. "Examine the text and images. See for yourself."

Eaaga looked at it. "Artifact. Your MAW is flawed."

Doland glanced at it. "Eaaga is correct. Artifact."

Soaa interjected, "W-we-we're in g-gr-great danger."

"Let's remain at full alert," I said. "At this point, hitting the Kicra is impossible because they're behind kapoks and other trees. If they attack, shoot to kill."

Eaaga frowned, then sat at a table.

Doland cringed, then gulped down coffee.

Croll stepped out of dome F. "I woke up a few minutes ago, and heard the discussion. Right now, the MCIT's are operating at eighty percent efficiency. In other words, reaching Isal could be difficult."

I cringed.

"Son of a bitch," Eaaga snapped.

CHAPTER NINE

When Doland finished his coffee, two Ditu, both with grey beards, strolled out of the jungle.

Soaa walked out of dome B. "N-Na-Naen Ot, leave us a-alone," she told the Ditu.

"Oron em et."

My lenses translated his words. "Leaving Oloo violates our sacred laws. You, Soaa, Xa Om, Ze Ma, and Wo Ra, must come with us."

"I-if-if we stay here, a-all four of us will die."

Naen Ot said, "Ab on ol." My earplugs translated, "Naax will protect all four of you."

Beyond Naen Ot, eleven Kicra crawled out of the jungle and stopped twenty feet behind him.

My earplugs updated my hippocampus. From this point on I would understand everything that Naen Ot and the other Ditu said.

Soaa pointed at the spiders. "Na-Na-Naen Ot, they're going to kill Adam and his crew an, any minute."

Naen Ot motioned with his hand. "Soaa, Naax will protect all of us from them."

"Na, Naax wah won't protect Adam and his crew."

Naen Ot pulled out a rope. "Soaa, you're wrong."

"M-Four, everybody, rush inside dome F immediately," I yelled at them. "Fane will take off when all of us have entered."

"Yes, commander," Doland murmured.

Everyone but me spun around, then sprinted inside.

"Adam, you're responsible for this," Naen Ot called out.

"I want Soaa and her friends to survive."

Naen Ot yanked out a knife. "You must die."

I did an about face, then rushed inside dome F. Behind me, the door hummed close. I spun around as all the domes joined, creating an upright disk, one of Fane's hull shapes. Within seconds, six Kicra darted around Naen Ot, jumped onto its transparent hull and held on while the ship rose. My heart pounded faster. Two banged their legs against the hull. Without warning, part of it cracked.

On my right, Eaaga said, "Adam, will the hull fall apart?"

As my mind raced, wondering what we could do if it did, I replied, "Hard to say. IT didn't have enough time to field test it under every condition."

"Shit, we're screwed."

"Maybe."

In front of me, four Kicra slid off the hull, their jaws twitching.

"Goodbye, assholes," Eaaga exclaimed.

I exhaled, trying to relax. On my right, the crack spread.

Eaaga aimed her arm toward them. "If only I could shoot the assholes."

"Better not." If she did, the beam would create a hole and both of us would be sucked out.

One more slid off, its legs flailing. Much to my surprise, the spider dropped into clouds, and vanished, obscured by them.

"We're two miles above Yerak," Eaaga said. "When will that Kicra give up?"

I flinched. "Good question."

Without warning, the creature lurched off the hull, venom shooting out of its mouth.

Eaaga clenched her fist. "Finally."

I bit my lip. "It's not over yet."

The cracks branched out. A popping, coming from them,

grew louder. The helmet and transparent protective mask came out of my suit and closed around my head and face.

"Adam, we should head for another compartment before the hull cracks open," Eaaga called out.

Sweat poured down my chin. "You go. I'll stay."

"Are you nuts?"

"I'm the captain. It's my duty to stay. There is a twenty percent chance my lenses can repair the cracks."

"If you say so." She rushed out of the room. A hatch whirred close behind her.

More fissures appeared. Soon tiny pieces broke off and were sucked outside. Outgoing air yanked me toward small holes.

Doland's voice came out of earplugs, "Adam, get out of there. Come inside compartment B. Save yourself."

"It's too late."

Doland's voice came out of my earplugs, "Everybody else is in compartment B. Come inside it now. I don't want it to end like this."

"Eaaga will take over if I die."

"Oh come on. Save yourself," Doland remarked.

CHAPTER TEN

The cracks started disappearing.

Doland spat, his voice coming out of my earplugs, "I don't believe what I'm seeing."

"It's unreal, hard to accept." Eaaga nodded.

Soon the last crack and hole vanished. I turned, then walked toward a hatch. It whirred open. I entered compartment B.

To my right, M4 commented, "Glad you made it."

I exhaled, trying to relax. "So am I."

Next to her, Eaaga remarked, "M-Four, you sound like you're reading off a page, like you don't care what happens to Adam."

My robot colleague paused, a vacant look in her eyes.

When our ship was two hundred thousand miles from Isal, Eaaga glowered. "Something, I don't know what, is blocking our scans."

"Keep scanning until you find a safe place to land," I told her.

Fane leveled off at an altitude of three thousand feet, then zoomed over a desert, a location in derm, one of Isal's continents. Below us, a ten-foot long scorpion crawled over a dune.

Eaaga squirmed. "What a horrible place to live."

I winced. "Yes. Is there an oasis on the laser Doppler screen?"

My co-pilot sighed. "According to it, there aren't any oases within a four hundred mile radius of us."

"Keep looking."

"According to the screen, a massive sandstorm is coming."

I cringed.

Within minutes our ship flew over it.

Eaaga frowned. "The storm is blocking our Doppler's scans."

My mind sped up, trying figure out how to deal with this unforeseen problem. "Program the Doppler scanner so that it creates a better map."

"Normally it could. However, primary cosmic rays are interfering with the Doppler's ability to do that. So far it's created useless coordinates."

I shook my head in disgust. "This is the first planet where those rays have interfered with that function."

"Yes. It's a fucked up situation. We'll have to deal with it for awhile."

"My assumption that Fane's MCIT's, spectrometers, and scanners could deal with any problem was wrong."

"I hate to say it, but that is accurate."

An hour later, at dusk as our craft flew over the Glorm, a jungle on Ba La, another one of Isal's continents, Eaaga announced, "This rain forest is huge, six million square miles. It will take hours or days for the Doppler to locate a good spot to land."

I winced. "It's much bigger than I imagined."

"There is more bad news."

My stomach muscles tensed up. "What is it?"

She groaned. "According to the latest QC Eight model, there are two flesh eating beasts in this area."

I shook my head. "Is Eight's probe superficial?"

"Yes."

I cringed. A superficial study was fifteen percent accurate. The best way to get the truth was by landing in that area and examining the surroundings. "Are Isal's other continents safer?" QC 8, a quantum computer, models could probe fractal and other shapes in jungles eleven trillion times faster than a QC Seven.

"No, they're worse. They're filled with one-inch-long flies. If any bite, you end up with malaria or another type of fever."

"Do any of those insects live in Glorm?"

She exhaled. "No. There are twenty-two insect species in the Glorm. All of them, beetles, ants and others are harmless."

"Is this a superficial probe?"

"Yes."

I rubbed my chin. "Did QC Eight's other probes indicate how likely it would be that there are any dangerous insects, species with bites that are lethal?"

"Model A, a rough prediction, indicates that there is a nine percent chance that those kinds live in the Glorm."

"Nine percent will have to do."

"Yes sir."

I contacted M4 through my lenses. "Did you see the latest prediction, the one Eaaga and I were talking about?"

The android's face appeared in my contact lens. "Affirmative."

"Do you think nine percent is accurate?"

Her white eyes turned pink, indicating that she was analyzing data. "That's hard to say because a safe spot is too far away to probe accurately. After the ship touches down, I can examine the location thoroughly with my MAW."

I clenched my teeth. "Understood."

Soaa, Xa Om, Ze Ma and Wo Ra appeared in my lenses, to the right of M4. "Soaa, Xa Om, Ze Ma and Wo Ra, we need to give you contact lenses, then show you how to operate them. It's possible that everybody might have to communicate silently because we're in a dangerous part of the Glorm. Since our lenses are unreliable, M-Four will teach all four of you how to use hand signals."

"L-le-lenses? Using them and and the signals will be a a challenge," Soaa said. "However, if we're making too much noise, the four of us will probably use our body odors to talk to each other."

I paused, amazed that they used the odors to speak with each other.

M4 gave all four of them lenses.

After all four of them put in their lenses, Xa Om commented, "Le-len-lenses? They ar-are tiny, feel uncomfortable."

Soaa turned to Xa Om. "Un-uncomfortable? Be—what is the word? Be pa-patient. They are helpful tools."

Xa Om paused. "He-he-helpful? Maybe."

Ze Ma flinched. "How you say . . . unusual? Xa Om is right. They do feel like that."

Wo Ra grinned. "Unusual? Mother, they will help us."

M4 said, "Wo Ra, your attitude is beneficial."

The girl nodded. "Ben-Beneficial? Wow, my vision is filled with numbers and other. What is that phrase? Fascinating stuff."

"Some of the stuff are probability graphs," M4 explained.

Ze Ma winced. "What? What is a graph?"

"It tells you which option is better."

Ze Ma disagreed. "Using our body fragrances to speak to each other is easier."

I blinked, surprised by her comment regarding the fragrances.

M4 ignored Ze Ma's remark and paid attention to Wo Ra. "Wo Ra, you're stuttering a lot more. Did moving to another planet scare you?"

"Ye-yes."

M4, Wo Ra and her friend's live videos vanished and were replaced by Croll's live video. He frowned. "Adam, I've updated two of Fane's MCIT's. That will make it easier to chart forty percent of the Glorm. Three hours ago they could only map five percent of it."

I thanked him. His video faded and was replaced by a recent nano robot probe. It scrolled. Twenty minutes ago, Soaa along with her family inhaled microscopic androids, some of Fane's new tools. Within seconds, the androids examined all of these new passenger's central nervous systems, organized many facts about their past, and sent the results into my lenses.

When Ze Ma was seven years old she figured out what nearby kapoks were saying. According to them, her body's candlewood scent was strong. As a result, they felt she was an intruder. Within a month, she knew how to control some of her body's odor. Then she used the scent to inform the kapoks that she was friendly and wasn't going to destroy them. Knowing this, the kapoks told her where edible roots were.

Nineteen evenings later, she learned how to organize the weak electrical signals that her body emitted with her mother's help. During the next few weeks, she sent hundreds of those signals to adjacent strangler figs. The figs responded and told her they would point out when dangerous beasts were approaching.

I paused, amazed by her skill. This information vanished and was replaced by more.

When Xa Om was five years old, he felt a tingling, a new sensation. Within days, he realized that nearby lupuna were using weak electrical signals to speak to him. He told his mother about it. She pointed out that he had discovered how to communicate with lupuna at an early age, years before many other children did.

I paused. "Xa Om, it's great that you can communicate

with lupuna."
    He thanked me.

CHAPTER ELEVEN

Fane came to rest in a small open space, a spot in the Glorm. Within seconds, its hull separated into eleven spheres. All of them turned into domes. Soon all eleven rearranged themselves in a circle, a settlement I called Homad.

Everybody stepped out of dome A.

"There are edible mushrooms nearby, six hundred yards from here," M4 said.

Eaaga rubbed her belly. "Good. I'm starving."

"Soaa, M-Four, Eaaga, and Doland, come with me," I said. "We need to gather some and take them back to Homad." I turned to the android. "M-Four, can you transport us to that area?"

"No, for unknown reasons, my body can't morph into that vehicle. The only thing it can do is change into different humanoid shapes. "

Eaaga scowled. "Not again. M-Four, what is the matter with you? I'm sick of this."

My neck muscles tightened. "Eaaga, calm down."

"I'm tired of failure. M-Four was supposed to be flawless."

"Stop complaining. That's an order."

"Yes chief," she snapped.

"M-Four, when will you be able to change into an APUT?" I asked.

"At this point, undetermined. My MAW is probing my skin and internal bio-circuits, trying to come up with an answer."

My jaw muscles tensed up. Our group departed.

After passing towering wimba, trees in the poorly lit jungle, our group came upon a small patch of mushrooms. Tiny boxes popped out of our belts, then expanded and started hovering. We placed the fungi in them.

A few minutes later, I said, "We need more mushrooms. These will only feed four members of our crew for a couple of days." In my lenses, text and percentages that were imported from my WMS scrolled. "These are edible."

Eaaga grabbed one and stuck in her mouth. "They taste odd."

Doland scowled. "Odd is acceptable. They're filled with Vitamin C and D."

"Ma most of the surrounding huicungo trees are giving off electrical charges, an event that never took place on Yerak," Soaa commented.

"Are you saying that huicungo were one of the few tree species on Yerak that didn't give off electrical charges?" M4 asked.

"Y-ye-yes, I was saying that."

"Why are these giving them off?"

"I-I don't know why."

"Soaa, your English has improved," I noted.

"Th-thanks. En-eng-English is an engrossing language. I say-say that because it's based on sound, esoteric references, clichés, and images."

"It is engrossing," M4 said.

"I hate this jungle. It's too hot," Eaaga snapped.

M4 pointed to a clearing nearby. "There is another mushroom patch nearby. It's only two hundred yards west of us."

I lead the way. "Let's go."

After hiking between huicungo, Doland pointed ahead.

"About twenty ferns are moving to the left."

"I don't believe it," Eaaga called out. She glanced in that direction. "It's dark, hard to see clearly."

"I know what I saw."

I blinked. "They're not moving now."

"They stopped," Doland snapped.

Eaaga sighed. "Moving? That's ridiculous. Anyway, I'm hungry."

Soaa stepped beside me. "El-electrical charges are coming from every direction. There are so many that I can't understand what any trees are saying."

Doland scowled at her. "Soaa, I've never understood how you or any other Ditu perceive the world. Although I wish I felt those electrical charges, it hasn't happened. At any rate, it amazes me that our lenses allow us to communicate with you and your friends at all."

"Th-they amaze me as well."

Eaaga scowled. "The big question is did the ferns move?"

"Like I said, I know what I saw," Doland exclaimed.

Eaaga shook her head. "Doland, the trees or underbrush are giving off hallucinatory fumes. As a result, you're seeing things that aren't there."

"I'm sticking to my story."

Eaaga wiped sweat off her brow. "My suit has broken down. It won't cool me off. Shit."

"Wh-when I was on Yerak, understanding ferns and some lupuna electrical charges and responding to these plants was a great idea. Sometimes they warned me about lethal orchids, poisonous roots and the presence of adjacent Kicra," Soaa advised.

"I've lost contact with Homad," Eaaga blurted. "What's wrong with my lenses?"

Doland flinched. "So have I. Has anybody come up with a well-informed answer?"

Eaaga scowled. "Not me. This is horrible."

"Not at this point," M4 replied. "My MAW is analyzing the issue."

"I don't know why either," I said. "More importantly, we're starving. Let's find the mushrooms."

Doland bit his lip. "Yes commander." Our group marched.

Soon we came upon them, grabbed many, placed the fungi in our boxes, then departed. Much to my surprise, the surrounding mist became thicker.

"It's hard to see clearly," Doland said. "Where did this fog come from?"

"Good point," I said.

"Come from?" M4 asked. "Probability graphs related to cause and effect are inconclusive." The entire crew tramped forward.

Within minutes, our group halted at the edge of a poorly illuminated sixty-foot-wide gorge. I cringed. "This barrier wasn't here before."

"No it wasn't," Doland exclaimed.

"According to my latest MAW analysis, this is the route we took before," M4 said.

"Going on this journey was a bad idea," Eaaga snapped.

I winced. "Does anybody have any theories about how or why the surrounding area has changed?"

Doland shook his head. "None. Although I see it, it doesn't make any sense."

"My MAW has offered six probability graphs," M4 said. "However, since it doesn't have enough information, the results are inconclusive."

"M-Four, you're not helping," Eaaga spat.

Seconds later, Doland pointed at the other side of the abyss. "There are three humanoids on the opposite side. They're just standing there. They arrived a moment ago."

I squinted, trying to see through the fog. "I don't see them."

Doland sighed. "The mist obscured the aliens a second after I noticed them. They were five-foot-tall, dimly lit silhouettes."

Eaaga exhaled. "All of this is getting on my nerves."

I glanced to the right, then looked in the opposite direction. "M-Four, does your MAW indicate how long this chasm is?"

"Not at this time."

"Does it indicate that there is a narrower part, one we can hop across to reach the other side?"

"Not at this time."

"More problems," Eaaga remarked. "Adam, you should have planned this trip more carefully."

I glared at her.

She frowned.

Doland grumbled. "It strikes me that this is an odd situation. M-Four's MAW has broken down, our lenses aren't functioning at one hundred percent capacity, the landscape is changing, three aliens appear out of nothing and ferns are moving."

Eaaga glowered. "I hear you."

My stomach muscles tightened. "Let's go right. Taking that route might lead to a narrower part of this barrier."

Soaa coughed. "It-it sounds like a good plan."

We slogged on.

After passing hundreds of kapoks, our group came upon a fifty-foot-long natural bridge, a structure made of tree roots. We veered left and halted.

I turned to them. "I'll go first. According to my scan, it's only strong enough to hold one person. If two attempt to cross at the same time, it will collapse."

Eaaga glowered. "It looks shaky."

Doland pointed down. "Some of the roots are rotten."

M4 agreed with him. "Doland, you are correct. Forty-two percent are."

Eaaga scowled. "Crossing this is a lousy idea."

I glared at her, then started across.

CHAPTER TWELVE

I stepped on the opposite side of the chasm, then turned. Then Eaaga started across. Soon five roots broke off and plummeted. "Trouble."

I winced. "Don't look down. Keep going."

She blenched. "Very well."

I nodded. "That's the spirit."

She inched forward. I grabbed her hand and she jumped onto the rim.

M4, the last member to traverse the bridge, paused near the middle. Without warning, a snapping became louder.

"Watch out," Doland yelled.

M4 darted toward us while the span started breaking apart.

Eaaga hollered beside me. "She isn't going to make it."

M4 leaped.

"That's a long jump," Doland blurted.

I pushed everyone back. "Everybody, get out of her way."

They darted to the left and right. She landed on the edge of the cliff, and began falling backward.

I grabbed her hand.

M4 grasped my offered hand firmly. "Thanks."

Eaaga frowned. "M-Four, you never sound irritated. That bothers me."

The android shrugged.

Doland patted M4 in the back. "I've never seen anybody jump that far."

"Although my body keeps updating itself, I was lucky. A month ago, I couldn't jump more than eight feet," M4 replied in a monotone.

"Yo-you jumped twenty," Soaa said.

"Twenty-one is more accurate"

Doland sighed. "At any rate, you made it."

Our crew trekked and reached a bamboo patch.

I blenched. "This wasn't on my map before."

Doland glowered. "It wasn't on mine, either."

Soaa paused, her teeth clenched. "A-although these changes are hard to believe, here they are."

"Going on this journey was a bad idea," Eaaga snapped.

M4's MAW hummed, organizing photos, videos, particle scans, ultra-high frequency and audible recordings. "Eighty percent of the surrounding area, spots that are within ninety yards of us change every few minutes."

"Are we on a fault line?" Doland asked.

"At this point, I'm not sure. Unfortunately, for unknown reasons, my MAW's ability to answer that question will take sixty percent longer than normal."

Eaaga shook her head. "Once again, you can't answer a question without struggling. As far as I'm concerned, robots screw up too often."

M4 paused with a blank expression on her face.

I turned to my co-pilot. "Eaaga, quit complaining. We need answers, not arguments."

She glared at me but didn't say anything.

I bit my lip. "Soaa, can you understand any of the nearby wimba, ferns, or weeds' electrical charges?"

"I-I cannot. They are unfamiliar."

My stomach muscles tightened. "We need to get back to Homad."

M4 nodded beside me. "Understood."

I turned to Soaa. "It's easier to understand what you're

saying. Our lenses' translation software is doing a great job."

She offered a polite grin.

Eaaga glared at me. "My suit broke down hours ago. I'm hot."

I clenched my teeth, annoyed by her comment.

M4 seemed to sense my annoyance with Eaaga, "I will try to repair your suit wirelessly. However, that will take time."

"M-Four you take too much time to repair a lot of equipment."

M4 looked at her with a blank expression.

At dusk our group came upon another part of the jungle.

"The lupuna and dangling vines that were here before have vanished, and were replaced by palmettos," M4 observed.

Eaaga frowned. "It's hard for me to accept that any planet's surface could change that fast."

Although Doland glowered, he didn't say anything.

"We're tired. Let's bed down for the night," I said.

Everybody agreed. Tiny domes popped out of our sleeves, expanded, and our crew stepped inside them. If any creature or humanoid came within thirty feet of these structures, alarms would beep.

I ate a mushroom, climbed into my sleeping bag and dozed off.

Chapter Thirteen

In the near distance, a poorly lit figure walked toward me. When he was closer, I realized it was Abraham Lincoln. He scowled. "Our enemies are everywhere. We must defeat them."

I woke up, realizing the meeting was only a nightmare.

M4 touched my arm. "Adam, you look shocked. What happened?"

I described the event. "I felt like I could reach out and touch him. It was the most realistic dream I've ever had."

"Captivating. I don't know much about dreams."

I shrugged, rested my head on a pillow and went back to sleep.

At dawn, after gulping down more mushrooms, our team continued on until we reached Homad.

As soon as we entered it, we were met with a frowning Browna. "Adam, we lost contact with you eight minutes after you left Homad."

I described part of our journey.

Hae Lana paused with an irritated expression on her face.

Eaaga scowled. "It was a uncanny hike."

Doland nodded. "It sure was."

Hae Lana spoke up. "Adam, Eaaga, M-Four, and Soaa, several minutes after all four of you left, some features in our lenses broke down. As a result we couldn't send or receive email, 3D holograms or text messages to anybody inside or outside of Homad or call each other with our lenses.

Also, sometimes our RFL's wouldn't function. Although our lenses could translate the Ditu language into English and vice versa, our colleagues had to be within earshot if we wanted to talk to them. I'm studying the problem but haven't come up with a solution."

Eaaga glowered. "M-Four can you repair the tools that Hae Lana mentioned?"

"I just scanned everybody else's lenses and other equipment, am working on it."

I turned to the android. "How long will it take?"

"At this point, unknown."

"Unknown? Why?" Eaaga blurted.

M4 remarked, "It could be airborne viruses, solar winds or any number of things. This planet is huge and we're newcomers."

"Shit."

I placed my hand on Eaaga's right shoulder. "We need to calm down, not get upset."

Eaaga glared at me, then grumbled incoherently.

"Soaa, tell me more about your language," Hae Lana suggested.

"This is no time to talk about that," Eaaga remarked. Hae Lana, you should help M-Four repair our equipment."

I lightly squeezed Eaaga's shoulder. "Leave Hae Lana alone."

"Yes chief. However, don't blame me if this mess gets worse." She stomped off.

Hae Lana sighed. "Eaaga should relax."

I nodded. "That is accurate. Also, we need to know more about Isal. Soaa can you help us?"

"In-in the near future, when I translate more of the kapoks and other tree's electrical charges, I will."

"Soaa, how did the trees on Yerak structure their electrical charges?" M4 asked.

"S-some of their charges are five seconds long. Others are shorter. Different lengths are combined to create a letter. Different letters are combined to make a word. Words are combined to create a language that the trees call Aon."

I nodded. "Aon reminds me of Morse code."

Soaa paused. "Mo-more-Morse code?"

"That is an odd comparison," Hae Lana commented. "Morse code hasn't been used for millions of years."

M4 looked at Soaa. "Did all the palmettos, kapoks, other trees, ferns and other plants on Yerak use Aon?"

"D-did all of them? No. But all of them understood it. As a result, sixty percent of them used it."

"Soaa, at this point, for unknown reasons, my MAW's probes are inconclusive. When I was in the Disi, one of Laasp's jungles, that equipment discovered dangerous beasts, deadly plants, and toxic airborne bacteria three hours after my group hiked into that area," M4 explained. "As a result, my group knew where to go so we could avoid those life-threatening obstacles.

Right now, for unknown reasons, the only thing the MAW can do is offer probability graphs, ones indicating that there is a five percent chance that there are two dangerous beasts within eight miles of us, northwest of this location.

At any rate, it's too early to answer my next question accurately. Despite this disadvantage, I have to start somewhere. Do any of Isal's trees or other plants use Aon?" M4 asked Soaa.

"Do-do any do that? I don't know. However, I'm still examining Isal's palmettos and other tree species. So far I don't understand the faint electrical charges they are giving off."

I cringed. "Soaa, I was hoping that we could obtain better answers regarding how many dangerous beasts and other obstacles there are in this area.

Also, figuring out why this part of the Glorm along with the planet's surface keeps changing is a big priority."

"We-we must be, how shall I put it, patient. This is a sma-sma-small group with limited resources."

Hae Lana frowned. "Soaa, do you know how to send and receive 3D holographic messages with your lenses?"

"Do-do I know how? No. However, Xa Om, Ze Ma and Wo Ra are helping me."

Hae Lana scowled. "Soaa, the 3D holographic messages give off electrical charges. Did you know that?"

"N-no, I didn't know that."

Hae Lana glowered. "Can you use weapons?"

"W-we-weapons? No. However, Xa Om, Ze Ma and Wo Ra are assisting me."

Hae Lana clenched her teeth.

At dawn, after I asked M4, Hae Lana, Doland, Soaa, and Eaaga for their help. We hiked, searching for food while trying to understand why the surrounding area was changing.

As the group passed two strangler groves, both of them surrounded by towering palmettos, Soaa announced, "I-I've grasped some of the languages spoken by this group of trees."

I blinked, surprised. "What are they saying?"

"Wha-what are they, they saying? Two palmettos are worried that we'll find the originator."

M4 faced her. "Did they say what it was?"

"D-did they? They did not."

I paused, caught off guard. "Did they say where the originator is?"

"It-it's four miles northwest of this spot."

"My MAW can't locate the originator because it's too far away. In other words, it can't verify Soaa's measurement,"

M4 said.

Eaaga glowered. "What is wrong with your MAW? Normally it has a range of five miles."

"At this point, unknown. It could be airborne viruses or thousands of other factors. It will take time to come up with an accurate answer."

My palms started sweating.

Doland scowled. "We should search for the originator."

My mind sped up, trying to come up with the best solution. "I agree with Doland." About two hundred yards from us, due north of our group, a beast roared.

"This area is too dark and thick. I can't see the creature that is making the noise," Doland said with panic in his voice.

My lenses can't detect its size or location accurately. M-Four, have you figured out what is wrong with your MAW?"

"Microbes have shorted out too many circuits. I repaired the circuits six times in the last five minutes. Unfortunately they keep breaking down."

"Shit," Eagga blurted. "M-Four, I thought you could do a better job."

M4 glanced at her with a blank expression on her face. "Sorry to disappoint."

Eaaga shook her head. "Great, fucking great."

Soaa stepped forward. "I-I'll lead us to the originator by paying close attention t-to strangler fig's electrical charges."

Eaaga laughed. "Paying attention to them is a joke."

I looked at Eaaga. "We'll follow Soaa."

"Fine, chief. However, I think that doing so is a bad idea."

My jaw muscles tightened. "Duly noted."

Hae Lana snickered.

I faced her. "Hae Lana you've become more cynical since we landed on Isal."

"So what?"

I bit my lip. "Soaa, proceed."

CHAPTER FOURTEEN

Within the hour, our group halted at a second riverbank. Hae Lana stopped walking. "Something is on our left, hidden behind those lupuna. Can anybody else hear its breathing?"

Soaa stopped to listen. "H-hear it? No."

I strained to hear the breathing, too. "Not me. Are you sure something is breathing? The only thing I hear is the sound of our footsteps."

Hae Lana glowered at us. "Yes, I am sure."

I stood closer to Soaa. "Are the surrounding trees talking about the breathing?"

"T-talking about it? No, the lupuna are saying that our footsteps are loud."

Eaaga sighed. "This is fucking lousy."

I took out my weapon. "Proceed with caution. If necessary, fire at will."

Hae Lana clenched her teeth and our group slogged on.

Thirty minutes later, we came upon a small clearing. In it, flies on three four-foot-tall statues of humanoids—sepia beings whose faces were mostly destroyed by erosion—took off.

Hae Lana touched one. "I've never seen anything like these sculptures before."

Soaa looked at Hae Lana. "Sc-sculpture? What does it mean?"

I was surprised by her lack of knowledge. "It's a work of art."

Soaa turned to face me. "S-several Ditu have gathered ka-pok branches and carved them, creating necklaces and ear-rings. Is that art?"

I nodded. "Yes."

M4 disrupted our conversation. "According to my MAW's 3D hologram, eight seconds ago, a creature asked a palmetto to spray amoebas onto my MAW. The tree did. As a result, my MAW couldn't spot the creature. Then I repaired the de-vice. Fifteen seconds later it detected the creature, a two-leg-ged, six-foot-tall carnivore, one I call a Teog."

Eaaga sighed. "M-Four, your MAW is offering fake re-sults."

"The results are genuine."

Eaaga chuckled. "Yeah right. And we're still on Laasp."

I gave Eaaga a stern look. "Your comments aren't helping."

"Sorry chief, we've got to be accurate."

Doland's brow knitted together. "I don't recognize the hi-eroglyphics on these alien figures."

"The hieroglyphics aren't on my databases. My MAW just scanned them, stored that information and organized it. There is a four percent chance that it might be able to determine who these aliens are and where they came from," said M4.

I sighed. "It's a start."

"Who cares about the hieroglyphics?" Eaaga blurted. "Let's find out if there are any predators or lethal plants nearby."

"Finding them is our second priority. The first one is to lo-cate the originator," I said, firmly.

Hae Lana scowled. "The originator is a joke."

"We need to search for it."

Eaaga shook her head. "If you say so, chief."

Our crew marched forward.

After climbing over six hills and crossing four stream beds,

M4 broke the silence. "The surrounding air is filled with millions of lethal protozoa. It's important to leave this spot."

Doland nodded. "Very well."

Eaaga scowled. "I feel fine. What's the rush?"

M4 turned to her. "If our group stays here, between two ridges, for twenty minutes, most of you will get a headache. Then your stomach will start to hurt. Within forty minutes, you'll pass out."

"Oh come on. It can't be that bad."

"There is a forty percent chance that you will wake up after passing out."

Eaaga laughed. "You're making this up. I don't have a headache."

Hae Lana was in deep thought. "Eaaga's statement is accurate. I feel great."

"F-feel great. Words I need to study more. The protozoa are giving off weak, hard to understand electrical charges," Soaa said.

"Soaa, can you translate those charges soon?" M4 asked.

"T-translate them soon? Hard to say."

"Let's go," I said. "If anybody gets sick, it's my responsibility."

Eaaga chuckled. "If you say so, chief."

"Eaaga, pay attention. Quit fooling around," I blurted.

She glared at me. Our group slogged on.

After passing hundreds of vines we reached a shadowy spot between thick bamboos.

Eaaga coughed. "I feel dizzy and my head is beginning to throb."

I blinked. "Let's return to Homad."

Eaaga sneezed. "It's not that bad."

"That's an order."

Eaaga spit out mucus. "If you say so."

M4 examined her closer. "Eaaga, you look pale."

She glared at the robot. "You're exaggerating."

"M-Four is not," Hae Lana spat.

Eaaga wheezed. "Listen to yourselves. You're overreacting."

Hae Lana shook her head. "We are not overreacting. Can you hear yourself? You're breathing slowly. Mucus is clogging your windpipe."

Eaaga coughed. "It's not that bad. It'll go away soon. Stop giving me shit."

I clenched my teeth. "They're trying to help. We're heading back to Homad."

Eaaga wiped sweat off her brow. "Fair enough."

Within thirty minutes, while pushing aside dangling vines, Eaaga stumbled and fell. "I have a headache. It's hard to stand."

Without warning, a creature, about six feet tall, barely noticeable in the dim light, rushed out of the shadows, then tore off the left side of Eaaga's face.

As my adrenaline pumped, the two-legged beast darted away and vanished into the jungle. M4, Doland, Hae Lana and I fired at the intruder.

"I might have hit it. It's hard to tell," Hae Lana called out.

"My particle beam grazed its leg," M4 said.

Doland sighed. "My ammo struck nearby dirt, not the target."

I looked down. Eaaga's eyes and mouth were wide open. "My laser beam grazed the beast's ear. At any rate, according to my lenses, Eaaga is dead."

M4 stood over her body. "Her passing might have been caused by a massive bleed out. However, Dr. Browna should perform an autopsy."

I winced. "Performing one is important."

M4 sprayed the corpse with a fast drying polymer, a substance that would slow her decomposition. Nanites came out of M4's waist, then formed a small platform. She grabbed our colleague's body, put it on the platform and we departed.

After reaching Homad, M4 entered a dome, then placed the corpse on a table.

Browna held her wrist-mounted molecular evaluator over our dead colleague's chest. "Whatever killed Eaaga did it by sucking thirty percent of her blood out."

"Are you sure?" Hae Lana blurted.

"Yes. Are you questioning my expertise?"

"Of course not."

Browna scowled.

"I've just never seen any creature that kills this fast."

Browna winced. "Now you have."

Hae Lana flinched. "Going to that area was a bad idea. Adam, all of this is your fault."

My back muscles tensed up. "Now that we know what we're up against, it's important that all of us should pay closer attention to seemingly random noises, unfamiliar animal tracks or anything that looks suspicious."

Everybody but Doland nodded. Although he glowered at me, Doland didn't say anything.

Hae Lana sighed. "Although I would like to search for the beast that killed Eaaga, we're not soldiers. In other words, it would slaughter us if our group looked for it."

Doland pointed at her. "We're not going to search for it?"

I blinked in his direction. "No, we're not. Rosk, Fesa and Yat were trained to do that. However, since they're gone, the only thing everybody can do is pay close to our surroundings."

Doland glared at me, but he didn't say anything. We went to our domes.

I entered my dome, climbed into bed, then dozed off. Minutes later, Lincoln stood in front of me and said, "We must kill all our opponents, a group led by Hitler." I woke up, covered in sweat, glad that the nightmare had ended.

At dusk, after the burial, Wo Ra turned to me. "I have translated more kapok electrical charges."

I blinked, surprised. "What are they saying?"

"Five one-thousand-feet-tall columns are called the originator. They are designed to create stars, moons and planets."

I paused, caught off guard by this news.

"It's a fairy tale. There aren't any columns here." Hae Lana blurted.

Xa Om appeared on the other side of Wo Ra. "Wo Ra, I love you but your story is unexpected."

"Xa Om, Wo Ra is talented," Ze Ma retorted. "You should listen to her."

Xa Om said, "When she grows up I will. Right now, she's only a daughter."

Wo Ra put her hand up, focused on something none of us could see or hear. "Now the originator is saying that Isal will break apart soon."

I turned to Soaa. "Is Wo Ra correct?"

"C-correct? Hard to say. Translating nearby kapok charges is tough."

"She is a youngster, not wise enough to make those kinds of statements," Browna remarked.

Goam nodded. "Dr. Browna is correct."

Croll frowned. "Although Wo Ra is a friendly soul, she needs to grow up, not take her fantasies too seriously."

Doland scrutinized Wo Ra. "She's is probably wrong. However, we should search for the columns."

"Doland are you nuts?" Hae Lana burst out.

"Your comment bothers me. All I'm saying is that we should investigate, determine if her story is correct. If it is, we might find out more about new planets, ones with fascinating ecosystems."

Hae Lana pointed at Doland. "You don't care if anybody dies on this wild goose chase."

"Of course I care. Your comment is stupid and thoughtless."

I spread out my arms, palms facing down. "Everybody, calm down. Tomorrow morning, I'll organize an expedition. We need to determine if the columns exist. Who will join me?"

"Not me," Hae Lana grumbled.

My back muscles tightened at her response.

M4 raised her hand. "I will."

"That's a start." I looked at the rest of the group. "Will anybody else take part?"

Soaa stepped forward. "An-anybody else? Me."

I sighed, disappointed that only two would help.

Hae Lana shook her head. "I'll go, but the expedition is a waste of time."

I looked in her direction. "Hae Lana, that's enough."

She glared at me and stomped off.

Doland stepped forward. "I'll go."

I faced him. "Doland, judging by your tone, you aren't interested."

He glowered. "Although Isal's plants and their relationship with the originator intrigues me, I'm a scientist, not a soldier."

My teeth clenched. "I know you're not a soldier."

Doland scowled. "To put it more bluntly, I don't look forward to fighting the predator again."

M4 held up two weapons. "Twenty minutes ago, I created several new pistols, an infrared spotter gun, I call the INSG. They're weapons that hit the target on the first shot." Each pistol resembled a one-inch-long hair strand. "Place it on the back of your hand. Then tiny fibers come out of it. They keep it from falling off." She gave an INSG to everybody.

Doland examined his closer. "It's tiny. I'll believe that it functions properly when it hits the target. Ever since we've touched down on this horrible planet our lenses and other equipment have malfunctioned too often."

I looked at Donald with my teeth clenched. "You don't have to go."

He sighed. "I feel safer around M-Four. She has quick reflexes."

M4 nodded.

The following dawn our group, M4, Hae Lana, Doland, Soaa and I departed.

"I-I-I'll lead," Soaa offered.

Hae Lana looked at her. "Why? You haven't done that before."

"Wh-why? In the last twenty-four hours, I've deciphered more of the electrical charges given off by lupuna, kapoks and palmettos."

Hae Lana scowled. "Are you certain?"

"S-se-certain? Yes. The lupuna and the other trees call their language Cogma."

I raised my eyebrows. "Soaa, what are the trees saying?"

"Sa-saying? Some are telling me that the originator is five miles north of us."

"Did they tell you what it does?" M4 asked.

"T-tell me? No."

Hae Lana glowered. "Why not?"

"Wh-why not? I'm not sure."

"Are you aware that it might be a trap?" Hae Lana snapped.

"A-a-aware? Sixteen palmettos didn't mention that. They

told me where the originator is and how away from us it is."

Hae Lana shook her head. "I'll follow you but this situation is messed up."

"Mes-messed up? I'm doing the best I can."

Hae Lana sighed. "Let's hope that your best will keep us alive."

Soaa marched forward. "H-hope? Wha-what does that mean?"

"It's another word for an optimistic attitude," M4 explained.

"Op-optimistic."

Our group swerved to the right.

"This is a new route," M4 observed.

"N-new? That is true."

"Soaa, all sixteen indicated that this is the best course?" I said.

"B-best? That is true."

Hae Lana glanced to the right and left. "This area is shadowy, full of underbrush and hard to travel through."

"Ha-harrd to travel through? That is true."

Far ahead, deep in the jungle, a creature laughed. I blinked and jerked forward. "That sounds like a monkey."

"M-monkey? It's a kapok."

Behind me, Doland blurted, "How can a tree make that noise?"

"H-how can it? Air rushed through holes in its trunk. Sap in the trunk compressed the air."

"Trees can't make that noise," Donald argued. "You made that up."

"Ma-made it up? I did not."

"Somebody else should lead. Soaa doesn't know what she is doing," Hae Lana said.

I looked at everyone in the group. "Soaa will lead. Stop complaining and pay attention."

"Yes chief. I should have stayed at Homad," Hae Lana said.

"It's too late. Pay attention. Otherwise, you can't hit anything with your ISG."

"I hope that it functions properly. Although its bulls-eye and trigger are in my lenses, this weapon is so new that learning how to use it properly will take a lot of effort."

I pointed down. "Take a practice shot at that slug."

A laser beam came off the back of her hand and hit dirt. "I missed."

Behind all of us, M4 remarked, "Keep trying."

Three more beams struck weeds. Hae Lana sighed. "Aiming correctly is difficult."

"Keep at it," M4 said.

Hae Lana turned to face M4. "You said this weapon would hit the target on the first shot. It missed the mark. Why?"

"Airborne streptococci have destroyed eleven percent of its bio-logic boards."

"That's a shit ass excuse."

I stood in her field of vision, blocking her view of M4. "Hae Lana, don't give up."

Twenty minutes later, after our group slogged through a gap between thick bamboos, we came upon a strangler fig grove.

Soaa pointed at dirt. "W-weak electrical charges are coming out of that. A Teog marked this area with his urine. Wa-watch out. Th-this predator may attack soon."

Hae Lana scowled. "My lenses haven't detected any charges. Soaa, did you make that up?"

"Ma-make it up? I did not."

Ahead, about forty yards from our group, the silhouette of what seemed like six-foot-tall creature, partially hidden in shadows, rushed toward us. Soaa raised one arm. A beam shot out of her ISG. Much to my surprise, the creature veered to the left and disappeared into the jungle. "I-I-I struck its neck."

Hae Lana came to her side. "It happened in less than a second. The only thing I noticed was the beam and an indigo shape. Most of the shape was hidden by leaves."

Behind me, Doland cleared his throat. "Soaa was lucky."

Soaa turned to him. "L-lucky?"

I stepped closer to Soaa. "Give credit where it's due. Soaa is quick."

Doland coughed. "Maybe." Everybody got a move on.

Soon we came upon a two-foot-long creature with a wide snout. Soaa halted. The creature wiggled its tiny ears and rushed beneath dangling creepers.

I blinked. "Is that species dangerous?"

"Da-dangerous? No. Judging by its electrical charges, we scared it away."

Behind me, Hae Lana said, "Adam, you've made a lot of mistakes ever since we left Laasp."

My jaw muscles tightened. "It's a difficult position."

Doland nudged her with his elbow. "Hae Lana, you should think more about what you're saying. Adam is more qualified than you are."

"Keep your mouth shut. Your words betray your foolishness."

"Look who is talking."

I stood between them and gave them each a look. "Let's pay attention to our surroundings, work together to reach the originator."

Hae Lana chuckled. "Adam, you took and take Wo Ra too seriously. She is a kid. This is a fool's errand."

I bit my lip. "Hae Lana, you need to be patient."

"I am."

My back muscles tensed up.

At dusk, tiny domes, the group's sleeping quarters, came out of our sleeves and expanded.

"I'll stand watch throughout the night," M4 offered

Hae Lana sighed. "M-Four, let's hope that you do your job correctly. Your MAW has failed too often. And it bothers me that I'm surrounded by bumblers."

I folded my arms across my chest, irritated by Hae Lana's attitude.

Hae Lana pointed at me. "You look angry. You don't like my comments?"

I glared at her but didn't say anything.

She grinned. "I've been patient for far too long. Now it's time for me to express more of my doubts. Any minute M-Four could break down. Or a creature might attack and kill us. You should have planned more thoroughly. If you did, we wouldn't be in this mess."

I turned away, disgusted with her comment "I'm doing the best I can."

Soaa came to my defense. "Ha-Hae Lana, why are you angry? We're alive and Adam treats all of us fairly."

"Because we're in trouble, the result of his poor planning."

Doland shook his head. "Hae Lana, you complain too much."

Hae Lana gnashed her teeth. Everybody entered their own sleeping quarters, ten-feet-by-ten-feet domes with carbon nanotube walls.

I crawled into my bed and dozed off.

Lincoln materialized, glaring at me. "You must help us defeat Hitler."

My adrenaline pumped. I woke up, then stepped out of the dome.

M4 was outside standing guard. "Judging by that shocked expression on your face, something is bothering you."

I exhaled, trying to relax. "It was only a nightmare."

M4 paused. "A creature is approaching."

I broke into a cold sweat. "The surrounding area is too dark. I don't see the creature. Unfortunately my lenses' infrared detector has broken down. Is the creature dangerous?"

"Dangerous? At this time, unknown. It's hiding behind strangler figs. It just turned and crept away."

I sighed. "Good."

"What happened in your nightmare?"

I told her about my dream.

"Captivating. The human mind intrigues me."

I shrugged, not sure what to say, and returned to my dome.

At dusk, most of us ate roots and leaves, food that Soaa had gathered.

Hae Lana's lips tightened. "These taste bitter. Are you sure that they're safe to eat?"

Soaa shook her head. "B-bitter, yes. Safe to eat? Their electrical charges indicate that they are nutritious."

Doland looked at her, amused. "Soaa, I can't get over the fact that you can't see but hike smoothly and don't trip over any roots or other obstacles."

"H-h-hike smoothly? Yes. I talk to the jungle. What is seeing like?"

Doland paused, a frustrated expression on his face. "You notice that everything has a shape, is usually a different color, and has a variety of textures."

"A-a-a thought-provoking comment. Can you tell me what a shape is?"

Doland glowered. "Each object is round, square, big, small, oblong or something else. Or it could be a combination of these. A kapok or lupuna is a combination. Does that help?"

"H-help? A-a-a little. Electrical charges create these shapes to some degree. At the same time, the charges tell me what the shape is made of."

In the near distance, hidden in the jungle, something rustled.

I flinched. "What made that sound?"

Hae Lana looked around. "It's weeds blowing in the wind."

M4 faced me. "According to my MAW, it's a six-foot-long four-legged beast."

"M-Four, it's artifact. Your equipment is malfunctioning. You need to pay close attention to these problems," Hae Lana retorted.

M4 ignored her. "The beast has stopped."

Hae Lana glanced over her shoulder. "According to my lenses, a fly has touched down on a leaf. There aren't any beasts nearby."

M4's MAW clicked, a barely audible noise. "The beast is leaving. I'll call it a Bolra for want of a better term."

Hae Lana shook her head. "A Bolra? Does anybody believe M-Four?"

I sighed, irritated by Hae Lana's skeptical attitude. "I do."

"I'm not sure yet," Doland replied.

"Be-be-believe her? Something is moving away from us. Un-unfortunately-ly I can't tell how big it is. Kapoks are in the way. As a result, it's hard to discover more," Soaa answered.

"Listen to yourselves," Hae Lana grumbled. "Soaa, you stutter too much. Everybody else, you're a ragtag bunch, lost in the jungle."

I exhaled, trying to relax. "Hae Lana, your negative comments aren't helping."

"I'm telling the truth. Somebody has to. I should be leading this group."

Doland looked at her sternly. "Hae Lana, as far as I'm

concerned, Adam is in charge."

Hae Lana glowered. "Doland, you're as foolish as the rest of this bunch."

At dawn, our sleep quarters shrank and went inside our sleeves.

Soaa was fascinated by it all. "It-it's amazing that our huts can shrink that much. It-it would have been nice to have them when I was a child."

Hae Lana chuckled. "Soaa, you're naïve, easy to please."

"Let's go," I ordered.

Our group slogged on.

After hiking over two valleys covered by huge Pallas — trees that blocked out most of the sky — Soaa pointed down at leaves. "Fa-fast moving electrical charges coming out of these ind-indicate that a Bolra is nearby."

"Unfortunately, my MAW can't detect the creature," M4 said.

Hae Lana chuckled. "There you go again, Soaa. Another screw up."

"Sc-screw up? The word is how should I say it, vague."

My stomach muscles tightened. "Hae Lana, knock it off."

She glared at me. "Somebody has to tell the truth, sir."

I bit my lip. "Be quiet. That's an order."

Although she glowered, Hae Lana didn't say anything. To our right, a five-foot-tall, four-legged beast, the same color as its surroundings, darted out of the shadows.

M4 fired. While everybody else jumped out of its way, the beast hooted softly, veered to the left and disappeared behind huge bushes.

Doland stood with his arm still raised. "It happened too quickly. M-Four, did you hit it?"

"I grazed it."

Hae Lana glowered. "I didn't get a good look at it. It was too fast."

My mind sped up, trying to determine the best way to fight this beast. "It moved so fast that I didn't notice it. The lack of light and thick underbrush didn't help either." I glanced into the distance, trying to spot the creature, but only noticed kapoks and other trees. "Is anybody hurt?"

"H-hurt? It tore part of my sleeve off with its horn. Lucky for me, it was a nothing serious."

Doland looked at Hae Lana. "You were wrong."

"Don't rub it in. We all make mistakes."

Doland frowned. "If we had listened to you, one of us might have been killed."

"Get off my back."

Doland glowered. "You used to be more upbeat. Now you complain a lot. What happened?"

"I usually kept my opinions to myself before. Then I got wise. You should do the same."

I stepped between them. "Let's keep going. We need to find the originator."

"We almost got killed and you want to keep searching for something that doesn't exist?" Hae Lana snapped.

I stared at her.

"Don't look at me like that, sir. Let's keep going."

Fifty minutes later, our group paused near thousands of tiny worms, invertebrates that were crawling over lupuna roots.

Doland sighed. "This part of the Glorm is as hot and gloomy as the areas we've hiked through."

Soaa looked at him, puzzled. "Gloo-gloomy? The air in this spot is filled with electrical charges."

Doland blinked. "To me and others this part is gloomy."

"Und-understanding what gloomy means will take time.

Bolra and Teog eat these worms. Pay close attention to our surroundings."

Doland sighed. "Gloomy means not enough light."

Hae Lana flinched. "I hate this area. The jungle canopy blocks out too much light."

"A-a Teog has arrived. It is on our left, about sixty yards away, hiding behind vines."

My adrenaline started pumping. "Will it attack us?"

"A-attack us? Hard to say. It's standing."

"My MAW can't detect it," M4 reported.

"Ca-can't? Now it's moving this way."

Hae Lana raised her arm. "I'm ready."

I pointed forward. "Let's head toward the originator. It's only a half a mile away."

Hae Lana glowered. "Won't it be harder to kill the beast if we're moving?"

"Ha-harder? It has stopped."

"Are you sure?" Hae Lana snapped.

Soaa shook her head. "S-sure? Yes."

I nodded. "Let's keep going."

After slogging through towering weeds for about thirty minutes, we came upon a maze of twelve-foot-long tree roots.

"Th-there are two Teog on our left, hidden behind dangling creepers." Soaa pointed in their direction.

Doland glanced towards the plants. "The only things I see are the creepers. How far away are the creatures?"

"How-how far away? According to a strangler fig, seventy feet away from us."

I winced. "Are they going to attack?"

"At-attack? I'm not sure."

Hae Lana spun around and shot a tree.

"Why did you do that?" I snapped.

Hae Lana blurted, "That might have scared them away."

Doland flinched. "Soaa, did it?"

"Di-did it? No. They're standing in the same spot."

Doland winced. "Are they moving at all?"

"M-moving? No."

"They're scaring the shit out of me," Hae Lana exclaimed.

"Let's get a move on," I said. The sun will set in a couple of hours. I want to camp in open space. That way we have a better chance of hitting these creatures."

Everybody else agreed.

"Su-sunset? That is the time when more leaves shut off because there is less light."

At dusk, our group came upon a clearing about twenty feet in diameter. It was located at the base of a fourteen-thousand-tall mountain. I said, "Let's camp here for the night."

"Ni-night? That is a time when more creatures hunt. According to grass, we're about an eighth of a mile from the originator. Our tribe must hike uphill to reach a gap. The originator is in a large clearing, not far beyond the gap. The grass says our loud footsteps and body odors make easier for different creatures to stalk us."

Hae Lana glowered. "Stalk us? That sounds like paranoia."

"Para-paranoia? What is that?"

"It means you worry too much."

"Hae Lana, you don't worry enough," Doland said.

Hae Lana glowered. "Doland, I wasn't talking to you."

Doland clenched his teeth.

When the first star came out, Soaa pointed at nearby bushes. "The-there is a Teog behind those."

I flinched while raising my arm.

"My MAW can't detect it because an unknown substance is blocking its scans," M4 explained.

"It's shocking that this predator is smart," Doland spat.

Hae Lana glowered. "Are you sure that the creature is close by? The only things my lenses detect are airborne amoebas and dust."

"Cl-close by? Yes, I'm sure."

Hae Lana winced. "I hate being around a beast that hides well."

As my stomach muscles tensed, I said, "Pay close attention."

"What the hell do you think I'm doing?" Hae Lana snapped.

I looked at her as I placed a finger on my lips. "Be quiet."

Her lips tightened into a frown. "It was your idea to come here, not mine, sir."

"That's an order."

She bit her lip as her face blenched. Then she walked toward the bushes. "If it rushes into the clearing, I need to be closer so I can hit it with my first shot."

"Cl-closer? If you're too close it can strike you more easily."

"The jungle is too dark and my INSG's infrared detector has broken down. If the beast darts into the clearing I won't be able to see it until it's a few feet from me," Hae Lana explained.

I gestured for her to come closer to the group. "Don't be a fool. Come back here."

"I know what I'm doing."

About five feet behind her, the beast stepped into the clearing, not making a sound. At the same time, its green leathery skin became shadowy, matching the surroundings.

M4 pointed at the creature. "Hae Lana, it's behind you."

She turned around to face us. "Don't play games with me. If it moved, I would have heard it."

As chills shot down my spine, the beast's tentacle — the one at the bottom of its jaw — reached toward the back of Hae Lana's upper leg.

"Oh my god. Look at its teeth," Doland whispered

Hae Lana flinched. "Doland, what are you talking about?"

"If one of us shoots at it we'll hit Hae Lana," M4 murmured.

I winced. "Yes."

The tentacle wrapped around Hae Lana's upper leg.

She hollered, "Something's got me." Without warning, the tentacle lifted her several feet above the ground. She fired in its direction, missing the target. "Do something!"

Our laser beams and ammo struck the beast's neck. It screeched. *Woooo.* Much to my surprise, it dropped Hae Lana, then spun around and raced toward me. As my mind raced, trying to figure out if it would bite my arm off, more beams struck its eyes. *Wooo.* I dodged to the right. Its claw tore off part of my sleeve. It veered to the left, darted into the jungle, and vanished, hidden by underbrush.

M4 took a step, then examined my arm. "It cut you," she remarked. "Even though the wound isn't serious, it should be treated."

"Go ahead."

She sprayed something on the injury. "This should heal in eight seconds. However, because the air is filled with mutated streptococcus, pay close attention to the laceration."

I sighed. "Hae Lana, are you hurt?"

She rose to her feet. "No."

Doland glowered. "Hae Lana, you're shaking like a leaf."

She glared at him. "No, I'm not. You're exaggerating."

Doland shook his head. "Your attitude doesn't fool me. That attack scared you to death."

"Shut up and mind your own business."

Doland sighed with an angry expression on his face.

Hae Lana took a deep breath and winced, then crawled inside her dome.

"I'll keep standing guard for the night," M4 commented.

I offered her a thumbs up. "I'm glad the beast's attack didn't rattle you."

"In the last thirty minutes I created a new tool, the TRS, short for tracker shape," she remarked. "It sorts recent photos, recordings, videos, and strange attractor shapes in this area. Every time any creature or sentient being moves it disturbs the surrounding air, creating those attractor shapes, and three D ripples in space. The TRS uses this information to monitor approaching creatures."

I nodded.

At sunrise, our group resumed the journey. "Air borne amoebas have destroyed my TRS's functionality," M4 said.

Hae Lana looked at M4. "M-Four, last night I heard you telling Adam about that machine. As usual, it broke down. Creating the machine was a waste of time."

"M-Four is doing her best to protect us," Doland remarked.

Hae Lana glowered. "She is doing a lousy job."

M4 kept walking with a deadpan look on her face.

"Hae Lana, be quiet," I said. "You're making it easier for Teogs and other beasts to hear us."

She glared at me. Soon we came upon a three-foot-long, four-legged animal, covered by grey fur.

I pointed at it with clenched teeth. "M-Four, anybody, is that creature dangerous?"

"Kill it before it does the same thing to us," Hae Lana barked.

Doland looked at it. "It's small, looks harmless."

The creature bit leaves off a bush and started chewing.

Doland nodded towards it. "See what I mean?"

"It's a herbivore," M4 added.

"Her-herbivore?" asked Soaa.

A Teog darted out from behind nearby strangler figs, reached down with both claws, then grabbed the small creature by its neck. As the herbivore wailed, a laser beam from Hae Lana's INSG struck dirt, missing the Teog. The predator dashed into the jungle and vanished, hidden by it.

"I was going to shoot the beast, but the other animal was in my line of fire," said Doland.

My stomach muscles tightened. "I had the same problem."

"There was an eight percent chance of hitting the predator without injuring the herbivore," commented M4.

"It happened in less than a second. There wasn't enough time for me to aim correctly," Hae Lana told M4.

"Hi-hit it? All of you tried," said Soaa.

"Let's move on," I told the group.

CHAPTER FIFTEEN

Not long after hiking around several boulders, beneath the jungle canopy, Soaa broke the silence and said, "I-I-I've discovered what some of these palmettos are saying."

I blinked, caught off guard.

She flinched. "Th-they told me that we're surrounded by six Teog."

Hae Lana scowled. "That's ridiculous. You made that up."

I shot Hae Lana a sharp look. "Let her finish."

She grumbled incoherently.

Soaa turned left. "Fin-finish? Yes. My body sent electrical signals to three strangler figs, asking them if they could hide our location for a few moments. That way we could reach the originator, not be slaughtered."

Doland scowled.

"It's a bunch of sh—" exclaimed Hae Lana.

I pointed at Hae Lana, cutting her off. "Let Soaa finish."

Hae Lana glared at me.

"All-all-all three said they just sent out electrical charges. The charges made it look like we had left this spot four minutes ago. Every Teog took off a second after that, headed to our right, trying to find us."

I exhaled, relieved. "Soaa thanks."

She grinned.

A hazy image of Dr. Browna's face appeared in my lenses. She frowned at me. When she opened her mouth nothing came out.

"Dr. Browna, what are you saying?"

Her face vanished and was replaced by dots.

"Dr. Browna, I lost the signal. Can you hear or see me?"

The dots flickered, indicating that our connection was interrupted. I told everybody else about it.

"I haven't received any calls, text messages or three D holographic memos from anybody at Homad since we left it," said M4.

"I haven't received any, either. I hate this. What a mess," Hae Lana burst out.

Doland blenched. "I'm having the same problem as M-Four and Hae Lana. We need to repair this problem soon."

I winced. "Yes. If anybody has any solutions, let me know."

Soaa stepped closer. "I-I understand what everybody else is saying about this because I am-am, how should I put this, having the same difficulty."

She rubbed her knuckles. According to my lenses, that gesture meant she was thinking about the problem day and night. However this new colleague didn't have any solutions.

Our group trudged on.

After trekking through a gap, our group came upon an eight-hundred-foot in diameter clearing. In the middle of it, fog swept past six one-thousand-foot-tall indigo columns.

Doland pointed at them. "They're arranged evenly."

"All of these structures are exactly twenty feet apart," said M4. Our group walked toward them.

I blinked, astonished. "Wo Ra was correct. The columns exist."

Hae Lana glowered. "She made a wild guess and was lucky."

"Your skepticism clouds your judgment," Doland shot back.

"My judgment is fine. Yours needs to improve," Hae Lana snapped.

I stepped between them. "Let's stop arguing."

Hae Lana paused. Her face was all scrunched up as she looked at me and said, "Are they machines?"

I looked at her. "Good question."

"Ma-machines? They're like boulders, not giving off any electrical charges," Soaa answered.

CHAPTER SIXTEEN

The entire crew halted and everybody touched one column's rough surface.

Hae Lana glowered. "There aren't any icons or letters on this. We've come here for nothing."

I squinted my eyes and examined one of the columns. "My lenses scanned this and the other columns and organized the information. At some point, I'm not sure when, they might be able to determine what the columns do."

"Adam, I updated my MAW moments ago. As a result, its electron microscope and quantum analyzer photographed each column's subatomic particle movement along with their molecules," M4 informed me. "The MAW will analyze all the photographs, all ninety-thousand of them, and try to determine what the columns do."

"The columns are quiet," Doland remarked.

Hae Lana frowned. "Alright. We've done our best. Can we return to Homad?"

I nodded. "Tomorrow, at sunrise, let's return."

Hae Lana glanced to the right and left. "This area gives me the creeps. Soaa, are the Teog watching us?"

"Wa-watching us? Unknown. There is lichen nearby. However, I can't translate their electrical charges."

Hae Lana shook her head. "That's great, just great. I feel like a sitting duck."

I placed a hand on her shoulder. "Hae Lana, pay attention."

She crossed both arms across her chest.

I glanced to the right and left, worried that a Teog might be hiding behind adjacent bushes, but only noticed dirt and small weeds.

At sun down, our group sat next to a column and ate roots, food that Soaa had collected from nearby.

Doland's brow tightened. "These taste like dirt."

Hae Lana sighed. "I know what you mean."

Soaa's nostrils opened wider. "D-dirt? Sniff them, then eat."

Doland paused. "Got it. That's better. They have a light sugary taste."

"Soaa, I'm glad you found these," I told her. "Otherwise, we wouldn't have anything to eat."

Her ears spread out. According to my lenses, that meant this meal was nutritious, full of vitamin C. "Ad-Adam, everybody, your body odors don't change that much."

I blinked, surprised by her comment. "They don't."

"Who cares?" remarked Hae Lana.

"My odors are usually the same," agreed M4.

The others paused, blank looks on their faces.

Doland blinked. "I could be wrong, but two of the columns have moved three inches closer to each other since we arrived."

Hae Lana glowered. "Are you kidding? I didn't notice it."

Doland cocked his head to one side. "It was a slow process, hard to spot. It might be my imagination."

I turned to M4. "M-Four, did you notice that movement?"

"No, I was studying my MAW's screen."

My mind sped up, trying to determine if the columns were made of pure carbon or something else. "M-Four, what have you come up with?"

"The surfaces are made of a combination of graphene, nano robots and another unknown substance. Molecules in the graphene update themselves every two seconds. However,

95

something on the column's surface has destroyed forty percent of the electrons that my MAW was and is sending out. Also, something has erased or smeared every photo. As a result, my MAW's probes are incomplete."

Doland glanced at her with amazement. "Destroying, erasing and smearing that many? That's unusual. No machine I know of can do that."

"It is unusual. My MAW's tools are taking more photos and creating more three D holograms."

"De-destroying?" Soaa asked.

"I don't like it. Are the columns machines, designed to hide something?" Hae Lana asked.

Doland paused. "They could be hiding something. On the other hand, I assumed that they're monuments, left by a dead humanoid race. In other words, my guess is they aren't machines.

I blinked, curious and baffled. "Is the unknown substance destroying, erasing or smearing them by accident?"

"Unknown," replied M4.

CHAPTER SEVENTEEN

A t dawn our crew departed.

When all of us reached the bottom of the mountain, M4 said, "According to my MAW, eighty percent of the kapoks in this part of the Glorm have moved."

I winced. "Are you sure?"

"Affirmative."

"How far have they moved?"

"It varies. I can offer a detailed answer when my MAW has organized more coordinates, photos, scans and three D holograms."

"Your MAW has malfunctioned," Hae Lana snapped.

M4 pointed straight ahead. "Those palmettos weren't there before. Do you remember?"

Doland frowned. "I remember. M-Four, you are correct."

"The-these palmettos charges are unfamiliar," Soaa commented.

Hae Lana looked at her. "Unfamiliar. Soaa, is that the best you can do?"

"The-the best? Yes. There are eighteen billion electrical charge combinations. Understanding all of them takes time."

Hae Lana glowered. "We need directions now, not in a week, a month, or later. Any minute a Teog or some other beast might tear us apart."

Soaa cringed. "N-now? I can't do it now."

Hae Lana shook her head. "You're a lousy leader."

I put a hand up to stop her. "Hae Lana, we need

constructive criticism."

She glared at me. "You need realistic criticism, sir"

My stomach muscles tightened. "M-Four, can your MAW create a map that will help us reach Homad?"

"Yes." She pointed to the right. "Let's travel that way."

Hae Lana shook her head. "This journey has been a waste of time. Adam, you should have mapped this area more thoroughly before we left Homad."

I winced. "That's enough."

Hae Lana glared at me. Without warning, she looked down, her teeth clenched and everybody slogged on.

In the late morning, we came upon a dimly lit stream. Doland scowled. "This is a different area, a location we haven't been through before. I don't recognize these lupuna."

"It is a different area," remarked M4. "Fortunately, we're at the halfway point. We should arrive at Homad tomorrow afternoon."

To our right, a silhouette, barely noticeable, rushed out of the shadows, grabbed Doland's neck with its tentacles, galloped into the jungle and vanished, hidden by underbrush. At the same time, laser beams from M4's INSG struck one of the predator's four legs.

Ammo from mine hit dirt, missing the beast.

Hae Lana spun around. Then she fired. Beams struck a strangler fig. "Shit."

"Th-that Bolra moved lightning fast, caught all of us by surprise," said Soaa. She turned to M4. "Our INSG's missed the creature. Why?"

"At this point, unknown. My MAW is compiling graphs, trying to come up with an answer."

I flinched. "Let's search for Doland."

"We should have stayed at Homad," Hae Lana blurted. "There aren't any soldiers in this group. That beast will kill all of us if we look for him. In fact, it might do that if we head for Homad."

I snapped at her. "Help us. Stop complaining."

Hae Lana sneered. "Yes sir."

"Like I said, let's search for him."

Hae Lana and Soaa flinched. M4 glanced to the right and left, a blank expression on her face. Our group advanced.

Within half an hour, our collective came upon hundreds of discarded snakeskins. In the far distance, hidden behind towering fucus, an animal hooted.

I flinched. "Was that an owl?"

"O-owl? Ac-according to these adjacent fern's electrical charges, it's a scorpion, an arachnid that calls itself a Flen."

"I hate scorpions," Hae Lana commented.

I ignored her. "Soaa, have you translated all of the fern's charges?"

"A-all? Only about thirty percent of them."

"Has anybody noticed a Bolra's tracks?"

"Fuck no," Hae Lana exclaimed. "The predator vanished without a trace. I don't get it. It should have left tracks."

To our right, about eighty yards from us, a dimly lit creature hopped from branch to branch, went between wimba and disappeared into shadows.

M4 pointed in that direction. "There is the answer. The Bolra travels between trees and doesn't touch the ground. Finding it will be difficult."

I clenched my teeth.

"Di-didn't land on the ground. A capable predator," Soaa remarked.

"We're in big trouble," Hae Lana commented.

Twenty minutes later, I held my arm up to stop the group. "We need more help or we'll never locate Doland. Let's head for Homad."

"I'm all for that," Hae Lana exclaimed.

At dusk, our group set up camp. Hae Lana sighed. "I wish we had reached Homad. I hate this part of the Glorm."

M4 stepped forward. "I'll stand watch until morning."

Hae Lana glowered. "M-Four, although your ability to protect our group used to make me feel safe, my guess is that one of these predators could destroy you easily, then kill us in seconds."

Chills ran down my spine. "Everybody but M-Four must get as much sleep as possible or else we'll never reach Homad."

"G-get as much as possible. I agree," said Soaa.

Domes came out of our sleeves and expanded.

I climbed inside mine, then dozed off.

Lincoln walked up to me. "You're a stranger, somebody in an odd costume. Are you going to fight with us or not?"

My stomach muscles tightened. "I don't know much about your enemy. Who are they?"

"They're inferior to us. We must seize their land."

I woke up beneath a starlit sky with my heart pounding. I stood and left my dome. "I had another nightmare."

M4 spoke with a vacant look in her eyes, "Tell me about it."

"It's similar to others I've had before." That empty expression in her eyes made me feel that she didn't care about my statement.

"Do you know what it means?"

"Not really. It's probably random nonsense."

"When you're ready, tell me more about this dream."

"Thanks for listening." I turned, entered the dome, climbed

onto my bed and dozed off.

At dawn, our group climbed over a poorly lit hill. To our left, several six-foot- foot long orange worms spat blue liquid onto leaves.

I winced, then pointed at them. "Are they dangerous?" I asked Soaa.

"Da-dangerous? According to several adjacent palmettos, they are harmless."

I exhaled, relieved.

Hae Lana rolled her eyes. "Soaa, are you sure? As far as I'm concerned, your ability to communicate with trees is over-rated."

"S-s-sure? I am. Your negative state of mind hinders your ability to understand others."

"Better get used to it. That's the way I am."

I cut their conversation short. "Let's focus on reaching Ho-mad, not trade insults."

"Ad-Adam, everybody else, your body odors haven't changed in the last few days. If they did kapoks and other trees could tell some or all of you where Bolra and other crea-tures are and what they are doing. In-in other words, I'm one person. Your help would make it easier for our group to s-sur-survive."

I blinked, surprised. "I'll try to do something about it. However, my suit isn't designed for this and I haven't been trained to do it."

Hae Lana mumbled incoherently.

M4 paused, a deadpan expression on her face. "It takes time for my processors and nano robots to reach that goal."

All of us tramped on.

"Ac-according to five nearby palmettos, our loud footsteps are attracting Teog."

Hae Lana shook her head. "Soaa, your remarks regarding

palmetto's electrical charges are ridiculous. Do you expect me to believe your comments?"

"Hae Lana, pay attention to her remarks. Fire at will."

She glowered. "If you say so, sir."

"Hae Lana, your impatience is a liability," commented M4.

This colleague glared at our robot colleague.

"Th-there are tiny insects on my arm."

I flinched. "Are they biting you?"

"Y-yes. Now my skin itches."

My mind sped up, wondering if they were lethal. "Soaa, what do any kapoks or other trees say about them?"

"S-say about them? According to several kapoks, these bugs, are a species called babans. They lay thousands of eggs on your skin. Destroy the eggs immediately or they will hatch in a few seconds and bite you."

M4 sprayed everybody. "This molecular deconstruct rips the eggs open in three seconds. They will die soon, killed by airborne viruses."

Hae Lana glowered, then scratched her neck. "The bites hurt. That deconstruct better work soon or else I won't be able to kill a Teog, a Bolra or anything else with my INSG."

To our left, a Bolra rushed out from behind towering ferns.

M4 pointed at it. "Look out."

Hae Lana tripped. "Shit."

Laser beams came out of M4's RFL. The beast screeched. *Eommm.*

I flinched while my ammo grazed its ear. The creature raced by me.

I spun around while it darted into the jungle. As my heart pounded harder, the creature rushed into thick mist. "I can't see it anymore. Is it coming back?"

"Come-coming back? According to three palmettos, it's circling us, waiting for the best moment to strike."

Hae Lana stood, blenching. "It probably left because it's wounded."

"Ac-according to the palmettos, the wound is superficial."

"We're too close to ferns and other plants. It could sneak up on us. There is a clear, ten-foot wide path ahead. Hike toward that," I said.

Hae Lana paused, her eyebrows were knitted together. All of us jogged in that direction.

CHAPTER EIGHTEEN

On our right, somewhere in the fog, a twig snapped. Hae Lana shuddered. "What made that noise?"

"My MAW's photos indicate that a six-inch long fly bit a twig."

Hae Lana flinched. "I hope that fly doesn't bite us."

"Ac-according to a wimba, a Bolra is twenty-feet behind us, stalking our crew."

Hae Lana scowled, then glanced over her shoulder. "I can't see or hear the predator."

My adrenaline pumped faster. "Hae Lana, fire at will."

She clenched her teeth, looked straight ahead and our group continued on.

To our left, a purple owl touched down on a branch. Soon it raised its head and gulped down a scorpion.

I pointed at it. "What is that called?"

"Ca-called? According to a huicungo it's an Oteb."

"It resembles a winged Gila monster. It stinks," Hae Lana said.

On our right, a striped parakeet landed on one of a gigantic orchid's petals. The bird took a few steps. Without warning, the flower snapped shut.

"That was quick," Hae Lana blurted. "That bird never had a chance."

"Affirmative, no chance," M4 remarked in a flat tone.

Ahead faraway, a squawking became louder.

I winced. "What's making that awful noise?"

"Ac-according to a shiringas, it's a rubber tree, called Ceto, a species that is similar to a leech, is."

Hae Lana frowned. "How big is a Ceto?"

"E-e-eight feet long."

Hae Lana shuddered. "Let's stay away from it."

I winced. "Good idea. Everybody, veer to the right."

"Un-unlike a leech, the Ceto spits lethal venom."

"Horrible," Hae Lana exclaimed.

"Pay attention to your surroundings," I snapped.

Hae Lana bit her lip as everybody slogged on.

Browna's hazy face appeared in my lenses. "We haven't—" Her voice faded and was replaced by static.

I turned to the group. "M-Four, everybody, Browna tried to call me. For unknown reasons, the call ended. Does anybody know why?"

M4 stepped forward. "I received that call, but don't know why it stopped."

Hae Lana glowered. "Adam, the same thing happened to me. I can't figure out why the connection was lousy."

"Lo-lousy? I haven't figured out how to-to use that too-tool."

At dusk our group halted between sabal palmettos. "Let's camp here for the night," I said.

Hae Lana shook her head. "We should have reached Homad by now. Something is wrong."

"W-wrong? That is an important word. Hae Lana has a point. Although I wish the adjacent lupuna had some answers regarding this topic, the only thing the-they're telling me is that our body odor makes it easy for the Bolra to follow us."

"I'll guard our camp for the entire night," M4 volunteered.

Within minutes, I dozed off.

My mother, who died when I was eight, grinned, "I'm so

proud of you. Your group will defeat Hitler along with his followers.

I woke, covered in sweat, then sat up. The dome wall became transparent, reacting to my body movement. Above me, stars twinkled. Was this dream about Hitler important? I put my head down and went back to sleep.

At sun up, Soaa handed out some mushrooms. "The-the electrical charges given off by these mushrooms, ones I picked recently, indicate that they're safe to eat."

Hae Lana glowered. "Although your comments regarding the charges are probably fake, I'm hungry." She plopped a couple in her mouth. "They taste awful."

I blinked, worried that this food might hurt my stomach, then gulped down the bitter meal.

M4 looked at me carefully. "Adam, judging by that look on your face, you don't like the Cep mushrooms."

"It's better than being hungry."

Soaa paused, then shrugged.

Hae Lana wiped sweat off her chin. "This jungle is hot. I'm sick of it. Gnats keep crawling on my neck and my suit has malfunctioned, won't keep me cool or get rid of the insects." She shoved the purple insects off.

"Your suit should repair itself soon," I told her.

Hae Lana glowered. "The sooner the better."

Our domes shrank. We placed the tiny objects on our sleeves and departed.

I turned to Soaa. "Is a Bolra following us?"

"Ye-yes."

My mind sped up. "How far away is it?"

"Six-sixty feet."

I cringed. To our left, several three-foot-long green roaches crawled over an orange leaf. Ahead, a foot long blue chameleon with huge purple eyes stuck out its tongue. A fly touched down on the fleshy organ. The tongue shot back into the lizard's mouth and it chewed the insect. Soon a stomping grew louder.

Hae Lana scowled. "What's making that noise?"

"An-an adjacent kapok says that a Binha is nearby."

Hae Lana frowned. "What is a Binha?"

"Un-unknown. The kapok wouldn't describe the creature."

"I can't see the Binha because it's behind dangling creepers," I said.

Hae Lana flinched. "I can't see it either. The ground is shaking. The creature must be gigantic."

CHAPTER NINETEEN

Within minutes, a fifty-foot-long reptile with a six-foot-in-diameter sepia head and leathery umber skin stepped out from behind the creepers. As it chewed, leaves in its mouth broke apart.

"It's a herbivore," remarked M4.

I turned to the android. "Why didn't our lenses or your MAW detect the herbivore recently or hours ago?"

"My MAW is organizing results. Unfortunately, I'm not sure why."

Hae Lana scowled. "M-Four, you aren't much help. Robots fail too many times. They're poorly designed."

M4 glanced at her with a blank expression on the android's face.

I glared at Hae Lana. "Knock it off."

"Everybody needs to hear my complaints. My objections are real. They won't go away."

My jaw muscles tightened. "Even if they're real, we need to solve the problem."

"He-her-herbivore? An unusual word. We Ditu call it a pono."

Hae Lana shook her head. "Adam, you're not listening to me."

"I am listening. Do you have a solution?"

She glowered. "If you had planned better, we wouldn't be in this mess, sir."

I bit my lip, frustrated with her comment. "Let's move on, head for Homad."

Soon after cutting our way through undergrowth, Soaa stopped. "Th-this vegetation says that our strong odor makes it easy for the Bolra to follow us."

"I can't hear the Bolra's footsteps.," Hae Lana commented. "It must make some kind of noise when it brushes against this vegetation. Soaa, can you hear yourself? You sound like somebody who talks too much and doesn't think enough about what they are saying."

"H-hear myself? Y-Yes. How-however, the Bolra walks silently."

Hae Lana sighed. "I don't believe it. It has to make some kind of noise. Damn it, I hate this heat."

Ahead, above us, on nearby branches, two-foot-long spiders chirped. *Eroo, Eroo.*

Hae Lana pointed at them. "They're hideous."

One of the arachnids dropped, then came to rest on the ground.

I flinched.

"That thing is going to strike," Hae Lana blurted

Without warning, it spun around, darted into the jungle and vanished, hidden in mist.

Hae Lana winced. "It's almost noon and this area is still dark." She drank from a bottle.

I nodded. Our group continued on.

"Many of the surrounding wimba are spraying a chemical, an alien substance filled with ions that destroys any messages from Homad," M4 said.

Hae Lana smirked. "Oh come on. They're trees. They aren't smart enough to do that."

"The chemical breaks the message's microwaves apart. At the same time, it scatters their electrons. As a result, the messages dissipate."

"Ha-Hae Lana, your cynicism makes it hard for-for you to

accept many truths."

"And your naive attitude is a blind spot. Somebody needs to point this out. Think of me as a friend who provides helpful insight."

"I-I-I want to think you as somebody who is providing that."

"Good. As long you think that way, we'll understand each other."

Soaa paused.

Hae Lana glowered. "Soaa, why do you repeat other's comments in the form of a question? It's annoying."

"Wh-why?"

I bit my lip and tried to calm down. "Hae Lana, you need to be more flexible."

"I'm practical. That's the important thing. I suggest you do the same, sir."

My mind raced as I tried to figure out how to deal with Hae Lana's attitude.

"Too many humans jump to conclusions and ignore facts. It's a huge problem, a dilemma they must face."

"Ha-Hae Lana, I only know two Aito. Do the other members of your race think they're as realistic as you?" Soaa asked.

"If they don't, they should. When I was piloting the Yean, I worked with two humans. Both kept losing their tempers whenever we talked about gravitational pull on the fuselage. They should have known more about how different G-forces affect a fuselage that is made of carbon nanotubes. This is especially important when a spacecraft is close to Zaol. I have to put up with too much ignorance when dealing with many humans."

My jaw muscles tightened.

"Hae Lana, you're getting upset," M4 said.

"That's not true. And I don't need any lectures from a smart ass robot."

Ahead, a Bolra rushed out of mist, then halted. I pointed at it. "Trouble."

Hae Lana spun around, her arm extended, ready to fire. "It's just standing there."

Everybody discharged their weapons. The predator dashed to the left and vanished, hidden in fog.

"Th-the creature is, how do you say it, a difficult target."

"According to my MAW, my beam struck its leg," M4 said.

I flinched. "If we go after it, the creature might ambush us."

M4 nodded. "Affirmative. We should remain in this clearing for three minutes."

"It's quiet," Hae Lana blurted. "I can't see it and my INSG can't detect its infrared signature. That's freakish. Normally, my lenses would make it possible to notice it. Is something on Isal affecting both of these tools?"

"That's a helpful question," I said and turned to Soaa. "Are the surrounding trees affecting them?"

"Af-affecting them? The only point three adjacent kapoks are making is that we're making a lot of noise. As a result, it's easy for the Bolra or a Teog to stalk our group."

My adrenaline pumped faster.

Minutes later, M4 reported, "According to my MAW, the creature has departed."

Hae Lana looked in her direction. "Are you sure?"

"Unfortunately, at this point, for unknown reasons, my MAW's maximum range is one hundred yards."

Hae Lana shook her head. "It could be one hundred and three yards from us and your MAW wouldn't detect it."

"Affirmative."

"Let's go," I said. "If we leave now, there is a better chance of reaching Homad before nightfall."

"A thirty-two percent better chance," M4 informed us. Our crew resumed the journey.

Hae Lana sighed. "Although I hate relying on a robot's pre-diction, it will have to do."

M4 glanced at her with a blank expression on the android's face.

I bit my lip, annoyed by Hae Lana's comment.

CHAPTER TWENTY

In the late afternoon our group came upon a fucus grove. "Homad is several yards beyond this," said M4.

"Finally. I didn't think we would get there before dark," Hae Lana commented

Above, on branches, small four-legged creatures with eyes on their paws chirped. *Ooot, ooot, ooot.*

"Their song is beautiful," I said.

"Ac-according to the fucus, these four-legged mammals are complaining, saying that the surroundings have changed in the last two hours."

I was baffled but curious. "What kind of change?"

"Le-let me think about tha-that for a second. They won't— how shall I say it—elab-elab-elaborate."

Hae Lana chuckled. "Their song is weird, meaningless."

"It doesn't match anything on my database," M4 said

Hae Lana scowled. "M-Four, you're supposed to be smart. Can't you come up with a more thoughtful response?"

M4 glanced at her with a vacant look in its eyes. "At this point, no."

"Robots are supposed to be quick-witted, a lot more than humans or Aito," Hae Lana said.

"Qui-quick witted? We Ditu call it soba. Hae Lana, you are angry."

"I am. Somebody spent a lot of money on robots. And this is the best they can do?"

I looked at Have Lana. "Your complaints are tiresome."

She glared me. "I . . ."

"Ta Hae Lana, your response was sh-short, vague."

"Tough shit."

Everybody came upon a grassy area, a spot between towering pallas palms. It was empty.

"Homad is gone," I blurted.

Hae Lana scowled. "There's no sign of it anywhere. How could it disappear without a trace?"

"My MAW can't supply any answers."

I turned to Soaa. "What do the pallas say?"

"Tha-that it changed."

"Changed? What does that mean?"

"The-they won't add any more information."

"That's just great," Hae Lana spat. "Our home is gone and nobody knows why. What's next, sir?"

Chills ran up my spine. "We set up camp, then eat. Soaa, M-Four, is that Bolra still following us?"

M4 scanned the area. "It isn't within one hundred yards of our group."

Soaa glanced to the right and left. "Co-couldn't detect it. According to the pallas, something scared it away four seconds ago."

I winced. "What scared it away?"

"A-a vibration."

Hae Lana scowled. "A vibration? That isn't much to go on."

I paused, trying to relax. "An electronic vibration?"

"The-they won't add any more details. I hope that detail is the right word. It's the best translation I can think of."

Compressed domes came out of our sleeves, then expanded.

"We-we're low on food. According to the pallas, there are some edible mushrooms in the near distance. I'll pick them. Anybody care to join me?"

I nodded at M4. "Go with her." Both departed. At the same time, crickets started chirping.

Soon a distant thrumming grew louder.

Hae Lana looked around. "What is that ominous noise? It's nerve wracking."

I winced. "It's coming from every direction."

Hae Lana flinched. "Yes."

My adrenaline pumped faster. "Whatever it is, it sounds like it's coming closer."

She jumped up. "It seems like this gigantic thing is hidden behind the surrounding trees."

My body went cold. "The noise is so loud that it's drowning out the crickets."

She glowered. "Speak up, I can barely hear you."

All around our camp, the pallas started glowing. I winced.

CHAPTER TWENTY-ONE

Soon the glowing diminished. Much to my surprise, the jungle vanished. Now both of us were on a beach. On our right, a huge ocean wave came toward us, broke apart and the tide rolled in.

Hae Lana frowned, then glanced to the left. "This doesn't make sense. What happened and why are we here?"

I winced. "No, it doesn't."

"Where is the rest of the crew?"

The beach and the ocean disappeared, then were replaced by the jungle.

"We're back in the camp," Hae Lana blurted. "Is my mind playing tricks on me?"

I blinked, surprised and baffled. "Yes, we're back in it. If it's a trick, it's unlike any I've seen before."

"I'm going to eat. If you figure out what is going on, tell me."

In the near distance, hidden in gloom, crickets started chirping.

Within minutes, Croll, Soaa, and M4 returned.

"Anything new?" M4 asked.

I told them what happened while they were away.

"According to my MAW, this area hasn't changed," M4 remarked.

Hae Lana burst out, "Nothing has? You're kidding me."

"I am not."

I blenched, shocked that M-Four's MAW hadn't detected

anything. "Soaa, have the pallas noticed any changes?"

"No. On-nly a vibration."

"That doesn't help," Hae Lana snapped.

I winced. "We need more information. Vibration is too vague."

Hae Lana nodded. "That's right, too vague. Soaa, come on, a few more words would help."

"The-they won't say anything else about the vibration."

"This is shitty."

In the near distance, all around our site, a cracking became louder. In front of us, two hundred yards away, the jungle shot up.

Hae Lana bellowed, "What the hell? Is Isal coming apart? Was Wo Ra correct?"

"Is-is it coming apart? Hard to say."

Hae Lana glared at Soaa.

Within minutes the rising jungle created an eight-thousand-foot high mountain. Then it stopped moving. Much to my surprise, our surroundings swirled and were replaced by the same beach.

I blinked. "This is odd."

On my left, Hae Lana scowled. "No shit. What is going on?"

My heart raced. "Where are Wo Ra, Ze Ma, Xa Om, Browna, Croll, and Goam?"

To my right Soaa remarked, "Har-hard to say. Tha-that is a valid question."

Behind Soaa, M4 said, "Adam and Soaa, my MAW hasn't come up with any new information regarding the other crew's current location."

In the near distance, Lincoln and nine men raced toward us, arrows in hand.

Hae Lana frowned. "What are these strangers doing?"

"An-another va-valid question."

I winced. "Be alert. If they attack, fire at will."

Lincoln stopped, then pointed at me. "Mab me."

A translation came out of my earplugs, "Sir, although you are an unusual being, please help us. Hitler and his followers will arrive soon. When they do, they will slaughter you and my believers."

My stomach muscles stiffened. My lenses offered a translated reply, "We'll try to help."

Lincoln scowled. "Your tone is odd. Yet you must help. They're mad killers."

In the near distance, tiny figures rushed out from behind a dune and sprinted toward our group.

Hae Lana pointed at the tiny figures. "Hitler looks angry. Does anybody know anything about him?"

M4 replied, offering a short history.

Hae Lana aimed her arm at Hitler.

Hitler halted about twenty feet from Lincoln and his group followed. His gaze fell directly on Lincoln. "Lincoln, why did you attack us? We want peace."

Lincoln whispered in my ear, "He is lying. He attacked us, then murdered my son."

I paused, confused. Who was telling the truth?

Hitler and his companions put their bows and arrows down. He called out, "We want to resolve any misunderstanding, stop any violence."

Lincoln murmured in my ear, "It's a trap. Kill him before he does the same to you."

I blinked, confused. "Alright, Hitler, I'm listening."

Lincoln placed the tip of his arrow against the side of my neck. He whispered, "Kill him or I'll shoot you."

CHAPTER TWENTY-TWO

Lincoln along with the beach vanished. Now I was inside my home. Several feet away, my mother who had died when I was eight, smiled. "I'm so proud of you. You've become the captain of a starship." She receded into the background. Now I was back on the same beach.

To my left, a thumping noise surprised me. I glanced in its direction, curious, then noticed Lincoln. He was face up on the ground. An arrow struck my chest. Laser beams struck Lincoln's friends and they collapsed.

"Adam, we didn't want to shoot them," M4 said. "Unfortunately they would have killed you, Soaa, and Hae Lana if we didn't."

"M-Four, you're quick," Hae Lana exclaimed behind M4. I only hit one of his associates. You struck all of them."

"You are welcome," M4 remarked before turning to me again. "Adam, did the arrow penetrate your suit?"

"No." I yanked it out and tossed it to the ground.

Not far behind M4, Hitler pointed at us. "You are aliens. " Suddenly, he, his friends and the beach went out of focus, then faded.

"No-now we're in a desert. Why are we here?"

I looked around us. "Compelling question." In front of us, dunes stretched to the horizon. Above them, two sun-like stars beat down on our group.

On my left, Hae Lana said, "This is crazy. We're moving from one spot to the next. If I didn't see it I wouldn't have believed it could happen."

"M-Four, can you explain these changes?" I asked.

"At this point, no. This experience is unusual, hard to interpret. According to my MCIT, the nearby stars are unfamiliar."

"Why didn't you use that MCIT before?"

"It was faulty, had to be improved."

"Unfamiliar. What does that mean?" The desert vanished.

To my right, Hae Lana frowned. "We're back in Homad again. None of this makes sense."

I blinked, astonished by these events. "No, it doesn't."

Dr. Browna stepped out of dome B. She glowered. "Adam, Hae Lana, M-Four, Soaa, where have you been? We lost track of you."

I told her about the shifts between places.

Browna glared at me. "That's bizarre, hard to believe."

To my left, Hae Lana glowered. "It is hard to accept, yet I saw it myself."

Soaa nodded in agreement. "I-I saw it, too."

Croll walked out of dome C. "Hae Lana, your explanation is important."

She blinked. "Yes."

Goam darted out of the jungle. "I overheard those comments and I'm trying to come up with a rational explanation."

I blinked, surprised by our disappearance. "Dr. Goam, are Wo Ra, Xa Om or Ze Ma nearby?"

"Yes. They're collecting mushrooms, should return soon. I warned them about Teog and other predators. However, they wouldn't listen."

Croll frowned. "Dr. Goam, Wo Ra has translated more of the kapok and lupuna's language and knows which areas are safe now."

Goam said, "She is only a youngster. Besides that, relying on a tree's language is a bad idea. Although Soaa and her friends say that they understand lupunas and other tree's electrical charges, I believe that Soaa and the rest of her friends are either fibbing or they are assuming that their fake explanations are real."

Croll sighed. "Goam, your cynicism is tiresome."

"I'm pragmatic. You should accept that, not pretend that Soaa and her friends know what they're talking about."

Croll paused with a concerned expression on his face. "Dr. Goam, although your concerns might be true, I and many others have to keep an open mind about the other crew's statements."

"I agree with Dr. Goam," Hae Lana announced. "He is being realistic." She stomped off, an irritated expression on her face.

My stomach muscles tightened. Then I talked about the originator. At the same time, my lenses shared videos, 3D holograms, photos and my comments regarding our journey with everybody who remained in Homad.

"Fascinating results, Adam," Croll remarked.

I nodded.

Croll added, "Did the columns actually move?"

"I didn't notice that they did," M4 said.

"M-Four, you didn't notice any?"

"Affirmative."

Croll glowered. "Why not? You're more perceptive than any human, Qio or Aito. Unlike us, you're awake twenty-four hours a day, seven days a week."

"My MAW was analyzing their surfaces, a complex procedure that made it impossible for me to notice it."

Croll hesitated before speaking again. An annoyed expression was on his face. "I want to know more. Unfortunately, Adam, upon closer inspection I realized that recent three-D holograms, photos and videos, recorded events sent by your lenses are hazy, useless."

I bit my lip, frustrated that they were useless. "Something

must have happened to them. Alerts didn't pop up during the journey. M-Four, did you notice any alerts during the journey?"

"Not at this time."

Croll frowned. "M-Four, Adam, anybody, are the columns monuments or machines?"

M4 answered him. "At this point, unknown."

"If they're monuments, who created them and why did they do it?"

"Adjacent trees didn't say," Soaa commented

M4 had a blank expression on her face.

"If they're machines, do they filter air, map the skies or gather data?" Croll asked.

"Unknown," M4 answered again.

"Important questions," I told Croll. "Answering them accurately will take time and effort."

"Dr. Croll, do you accept Wo Ra's explanation that the originator creates stars and so on?" M4 asked.

He winced. "That is a demanding query. If she is correct, then everything I stand for is wrong. However, because quantum mechanics is outlandish, it's best to spend more time thinking about her explanation."

"What does its outlandish nature have to do with her explanation?"

Croll sighed. "Quantum mechanics is counterintuitive. However, because it's accurate, most scientists have to accept the fact that it's real. In other words, although Wo Ra's explanation regarding the originator's role of creating stars, planets and moons is counterintuitive it could be true."

Goam nodded. "Dr. Croll, your explanation regarding the columns and quantum mechanics intrigues me."

To my left, behind towering palmettos, a faint scraping sound became louder. I winced. "Something is approaching."

Goam glanced in that direction. "It's probably Wo Ra, Xo

Om and Ze Ma."

A two-inch-long gnat flew out from behind them.

Croll smiled. "Dr. Goam, you were incorrect." A Teog rushed out of bushes, sliced Goam's head off with its claws, grabbed it along with the rest of him, dashed into the jungle and vanished, hidden by underbrush.

M4 and I fired. Our ammo struck dirt, missing the target.

"That beast moved lightning fast," Croll blurted. "By the time I figured out what it was doing, the creature was gone."

"It was fast," I said as my adrenaline pumped faster.

Croll winced, then pointed down. "There is spattered blood in the dirt."

Chills ran up my spine. "Watch out, the beast might come back."

Croll's hands began shaking. "I'm not prepared for this."

Hae Lana returned. She pointed at the blood. "What happened?"

I told her about Dr. Goam.

Hae Lana glowered. "Adam, you should have been more alert."

Croll scowled. "Hae Lana is correct."

M4 defended me. "He is doing his best."

Hae Lana snapped, "I don't like smart ass robots."

M4 glanced at her with a blank expression on the android's face.

"Yes, M-Four, I'm talking about you."

The robot paused with a vacant look in her eyes.

I stood between them. "We have to pay attention. The creature is probably nearby."

On my right, forty feet behind Hae Lana, a crunching sound grew louder. She turned around and fired at bushes, foliage where the noise was coming from.

Ze Ma stepped out from behind them. "Why are you shooting at me?"

"You should have told everybody you were coming," Hae Lana snapped.

"We've never done that before. Why now?"

I answered.

Hae Lana glowered. "Adam, you're losing control. I should take over."

"Adam is in charge, not you," Croll remarked.

Hae Lana gazed at Croll but didn't say anything.

I exhaled, releasing tension. "All of us are under a lot of pressure. We need to calm down."

Wo Ra and Xa Om arrived. "Wo Ra and I heard those arguments. Adam is correct. We need to calm down," Xa Om said.

Hae Lana mumbled incoherently with an angry expression on her face.

Wo Ra and Xa Om handed out mushrooms.

Ze Ma offered a tense smile. "Good. Everybody is hungry."

To my left, hidden in the jungle, something snapped.

CHAPTER TWENTY-THREE

Everybody jerked their arms upward, ready to fire.

"A two-foot-long mammal, a herbivore, is chewing leaves," M4 informed us.

Hae Lana glowered. "Maybe. Teog's are clever. It might be waiting to strike."

An alert appeared in my lenses, indicating that part of their scanning functionality had broken down. I winced, then told the others.

"Not again," Hae Lana spat.

"This is aggravating," Croll remarked.

"Adam, if you along with the rest of the crew knew how to communicate with kapoks and other trees they wouldn't have to depend on their lenses," Xa Om said.

Hae Lana sighed. "Communicate with kapoks. What a joke."

"A-a joke? I disagree," Soaa remarked.

"Hae Lana, communicating with them would he help you survive," said Xa Om.

"My lenses, quick reflexes and weapons are the best solution, not strangler figs, bushes or other plants." She walked off with a contemptuous expression on her face.

Wo Ra watched her walk away. "It is too bad that Hae Lana will not change."

Croll's brow tightened in concentration, but he didn't say anything.

Not long after dusk, I entered my dome, climbed into bed,

then dozed off.

My grandfather Nick smiled. "Adam, it's good to see you."
I nodded.

Behind him, my grandmother, Jane, wiped tears off her cheeks. "Scientists have said that a gamma ray will strike Laasp in two weeks. I'm scared."

My heart pounded. I woke up, covered in sweat, climbed out of bed, and left the dome.

M4 was outside. "Judging by that expression on your face something is bothering you."

I told M4 my dream.

"According to my research, dreams can be random nonsense or a technique the brain uses to solve a problem."

"I felt that I could touch my grandfather and grandmother."

"A mysterious event. Would you say it was more than a dream?"

"I want to say it was. However, if that isn't true, what was it?"

"At this point, unknown."

Hae Lana arrived. I told her about the dream.

She glowered. "It was nightmare, nothing more. Forget about it."

My stomach muscles tightened. "But it was realistic."

My colleague shook her head. "Two days ago, I had a nightmare. In it, my brother, who died when I was twenty-two, told me that all life on Laasp would end in five days when a gamma ray struck it."

I blinked, surprised. "You assume that it's only a nightmare?"

"It was a nightmare, can't be anything else. Like you've said, we should be alert."

I bit lip, annoyed by her narrow interpretation. She departed.

My mind sped up, trying to come up with an explanation that would convince her that the dream could be something else.

"Did Hae Lana's explanation bother you?" M4 asked.

I sighed. "She is probably right, it was only a nightmare. However, it was more realistic than usual. It felt as if I was there, in another place."

"Could it be a premonition?"

I blinked, surprised. "I want to think so. However, that idea feels wrong, as if I'm fooling myself."

Wo Ra emerged from dome F. "I heard that. In the last few days I have had many dreams. In two of them, my mom and I are standing on a cliff, one that is not in the Weon. In the sky, thousands of asteroids are dropping, bound for nearby canyons. The dream ends there."

I paused, weighing options.

Ze Ma stepped out of dome G. "Wo Ra, are you still talking about those odd dreams?"

"Odd dreams? Yes, Mother. I am sorry."

She hugged her daughter. "We must clean mushrooms." They departed.

I watched them as they headed towards the mushrooms. "I'm not the only one with realistic dreams."

M4 looked ahead of her. "At this point, affirmative."

Far away, a distant rumbling grew louder. I winced. "What is that noise?"

"According to my MAW, a dormant volcano has erupted."

My adrenaline pumped faster. "How far away is it? My lenses are only receiving static."

"Eight miles and sixty feet. By the way, poisonous gases are shooting out of it."

I blinked, surprised. "You repaired your MAW."

"Affirmative."

I broke into a cold sweat. "Will the gases come here?"

"According to my MAW's graph, there is a twenty-four percent chance that they will."

I blenched. "When will they arrive?"

"At this point, one computer model, a preliminary analysis, indicates forty-five minutes."

"Are there any other models?"

"Yes. Two. The second indicates fifty-one minutes. The third, fifty-nine."

Chills ran up my spine. "Our domes can filter out the fumes."

"True. However, another model indicates that the gas will be accompanied by volcanic dust. As a result, everybody but me might choke to death. There is a forty-five percent chance that the domes will eliminate the dust."

I blenched. "Will our suits eliminate the dust?"

"No."

My stomach muscles tightened. "There is another problem. My lenses can't send or receive any calls, emails or 3-D holographic messages anymore." To our right, not far beyond the domes, a faint crunching became louder. "In the last two seconds, my lenses have repaired forty percent of their scanning functionality. According to them, two Teog's have arrived, are hiding in the adjacent jungle."

CHAPTER TWENTY-FOUR

" A ccording to my MAW, that is correct."
I sighed. "Everybody is tired and needs to sleep."
"I will stand guard until morning."

I climbed out of bed, left the dome, and entered another. Above me, on its surface, volcanic dust blocked out some of the sky. Within seconds, the debris remover — DR — switched on and pushed the dust away.

M4 entered. "The DR is functioning normally."

I sighed. "Impressive. Are the Teog's still here?"

"No, they left twenty minutes ago."

I blinked, surprised. "Why?"

"My guess, based on two computers models, is that since volcanic dust partly clogged their nostrils, they wanted to find a spot where the debris wasn't falling."

I departed, entered my dome, climbed into bed, then dozed off.

Lorna, my ex-wife — a beautiful spouse who left me because she said I worked too much and didn't spend enough time with her — kissed our baby girl. Lorna giggled. "Isn't she beautiful?"

My mind sped up. "Yes."

Lorna grinned. "Tell daddy you love him."

Our baby, Jennifer, reached out and touched my hand. "I wuv u, daddy."

I sighed, grateful. In my contact lenses, news scrolled,

indicating that a gamma ray would strike Laasp in five weeks, destroying all life on it. Chills raced up my spine.

Lorna frowned. "Adam, what's wrong? You looked shocked."

"Yes."

I woke up, covered in sweat.

Twenty minutes later, at breakfast, Croll frowned. "I had a dream last night. In it, Dr. Mein, one of my colleagues, told me that the Pres Committee had given me the Silven, a prestigious medal because my star maps of Sirius and Aldebaran were far more accurate than those created by anybody else on Laasp. Much to my surprise, he pointed out that a lethal gamma ray would strike the Gamoren, the space station I was on within six hours. Then I woke up. The nightmare was astonishing, extremely tangible."

"Were you ever on the Gamoren?" I asked, curious.

Croll glowered. "No."

"Why not?" M4 asked.

Croll's forehead tightened. "I applied for a position that would allow me to work there. However, they rejected me, said my ideas regarding collapsing stars were flawed."

Browna winced. "I'm sorry to hear it."

Croll sighed. "Thanks. Dr. Browna, did you have a dream?"

"You bet."

"Tell us about it."

"It's embarrassing. I was in Oip, a jungle near the center of Fot, examining a corpse, one of nine, trying to determine the cause of death — COD. I loved the challenge, felt that if I could solve this mystery, it would prove that my theory regarding quantum tunneling in cancer cells was correct."

According to my lenses, Oip was one of the most

dangerous jungles on Laasp.

Croll nodded. "Were you ever in Oip?"

She glowered. "Why do you ask?"

He shrugged. "Just curious."

"Unfortunately not. Two of my colleagues were sent there. I was jealous, felt left out."

"Sorry to hear it."

Browna paused. "Three weeks after they arrived, both colleagues died."

"What killed them?"

Browna frowned. "They inhaled airborne ciliates, complained about headaches, climbed into bed, then passed out. They never woke up because neurotoxins destroyed most of their brainstem."

Croll's eyes opened wide. "Horrible."

Browna flinched. "Indeed. Thinking about it makes me sad."

Ze Ma arrived. "I woke a few minutes ago, had an ab-ab-absorbing d-dr-dream. I think that's the right word. In it, Xa Om introduced me to his son."

Browna's brow tightened in concentration. "Xa Om has a son?"

Ze Ma remarked, "No, he doesn't."

"Is he your husband?"

"Um, yes."

Xa Om rushed out of a dome. "I heard that. Five nights ago, I dreamed about a beautiful woman."

Browna smiled. "Xa Om, was it a pleasant dream?"

"Pleasant? It was mixed. Years ago, when we met, I asked what her name was. She said it was La Ra. Although I wanted to spend more time with her she turned, and walked away, an experience that hurt my feelings. A week later, I saw her talking to Mem On, another man. Eventually, they had two sons. Every time I looked at her sons, I felt jealous. Anyway, for the last three nights, when I was dreaming, La Ra and I married and had two sons."

"Thought-provoking," Browna remarked.

"I've never had the same dream three nights in a row," Xa Om said.

Browna nodded with an astonished expression on her face.

"Dr. Browna, have you ever had the same dream three nights in a row?" Xa Om asked her.

She flinched. "Never."

M4 stepped out of a dome.

I faced the robot. "M-Four, have you been listening to these stories about dreams?"

"Affirmative."

"What do you think about the fact that some of them are recurring?"

"At this point, unknown. Ask me later, when I've had more time to analyze them."

Wo Ra darted out of a dome. "For four nights in a row, I experienced the same dream. In it, I am standing in a snow-covered valley."

"Wo Ra, have you ever been to a place like that?" Browna asked.

"Like that? No. I have spent my entire life in the Weon."

Browna paused, a perplexed expression on her face.

The following dawn, M4, Soaa, Browna, Hae Lana, Xa Om and I left Homad, searching for Doland. Soon our group spread out.

"The undergrowth is thick. I can't see anybody else," Hae Lana announced.

"Stay within earshot," I told her.

"As you wish. But this whole effort is a waste."

"Waste? According to three wimba, an injured being is two

miles from us," Xa Om said.

Hae Lana laughed. "Are you kidding me? This nonsense about trees speaking is stupid."

"Stupid? That is a rude comment."

Before Hae Lana could respond, I told Xo Om to the lead the way for us. "We'll follow."

"I can't believe this, sir," Hae Lana remarked.

I looked at her sternly. "That is an order."

"As you wish, commander."

CHAPTER TWENTY-FIVE

Two afternoons later, our crew halted near a wall of creepers.

Hae Lana coughed. "I'm tired. It's hot and we haven't found Doland."

To my left, he stepped out of the shadows.

I winced. "You're injured. What happened?"

Doland replied in a raspy voice. "A Bolra grabbed my arm with its tentacle. I fell. It grabbed my leg with its tentacle and dragged me about eighty yards. I shot it in the belly. It bit two fingers from my right hand off. I fired again. It spun around, then dashed off. I rose to my feet and sprayed a bandage on my hand. Then I hiked, hoping it wouldn't follow me, but soon I was lost. Feeling desperate, I sat between three kapoks and waited."

I grabbed him by the shoulder. "Understood. Let's return to Homad."

Minutes later, as our group climbed over a ridge, Soaa remarked, "Ac-according to the adjacent huicungos, a Teog is following us."

Hae Lana scowled. "I don't see it and it hasn't appeared in my lenses. Are you sure that the trees are correct?"

"Co-correct? Quite sure."

Hae Lana glowered. "If I see animals or they appear in my lenses, I know for certain that they're close by."

I flinched, annoyed by Hae Lana's comment.

"Ta Hae Lana, ignoring the huicungos warning puts you

in great danger," Soaa warned.

"I'll be the judge of that."

Browna's hazy face appeared in my lenses. She glowered at me. "Can you . . ." Her face disappeared and was replaced by lines.

I blurted, "Dr. Browna, can you hear or see me? I can't see or hear you anymore."

Hae Lana sighed. "Another bad connection. What a fucking mess. M-Four, anybody, can you fix our lenses so they don't break down?"

To my right, the creature rushed out of darkness. M4, Hae Lana and I fired. The predator sprinted behind wimba and vanished, hidden by them.

"Te Hae Lana, it's important that you heed the huicungos' warning."

"The last thing I need is a lecture."

I clenched my teeth. "Hae Lana, you need to pay closer attention."

She glared at me. "Yes, sir."

In the late afternoon our group arrived in Homad. Ze Ma darted out of dome A. "Dr. Doland, you're alive. It's good to see you."

He offered a weak smile. "Thanks."

"I would like to give you mushrooms to eat, but we're out. Would anybody like to help me gather some?"

Doland volunteered. "Sure."

Hae Lana stepped placed her hand on his shoulder. "Doland, be careful. Every few minutes, I hear rustlings in the nearby jungle."

He shook his head. "My aim is improving." Ze Ma and he walked away.

Hae Lana glowered. "Adam, you should have stopped him. He will probably get hurt."

I sighed. "Understood. Soaa, are any kapoks or other trees warning us about Teog's or anything else?"

"The-they're talking about a vibration."

"Not that again," Hae Lana snapped. "Damn it, tell me what is making the vibration."

"The-they won't mention anything else."

My stomach muscles tightened. My lenses called Doland's lenses. Only lines appeared in my lenses. I informed the rest about my attempt to reach him.

Hae Lana glowered. "Damn it, I'm not having any luck either. My diagnostic software — AF — can't determine why my lenses can't get the call to go through."

I winced. Forty percent of the time AF — application failure notification — didn't work. We try could repairing the software breakdown.

"Mi-mine can't either. Is-is it, my fault?"

"It isn't your fault," M4 said. "Some unknown factor on Isal has destroyed AF's functionality. At some point, my MAW will determine why AF has failed and repair it."

Hae Lana scowled. "M-Four, in terms of repairing my AF, you and your MAW are slow. I'm going to fix it myself."

The android looked at her with a blank look on its face. "Go ahead, do it."

I bit my lip, annoyed by Hae Lana's attitude. "Soaa, Hae Lana, and M-Four, let's search for Doland and Ze Ma." Our group set off.

Soon we passed towering palmettos. I called out for missing members. "Ze Ma, Doland, can you hear me?"

No response.

Hae Lana sighed. "This area is black as night and it smells like shit. The branches make it hard to see more than a few feet. Son of a bitch."

On our right, a scratching grew louder.

I cringed. "What's making that noise?"

"You tell me," Hae Lana spat,

"Ac-according to a strangler fig, a Bolra is chewing something."

I winced. "How far away is the creature?"

"Nine-ninety yards."

"Is it on our left, our right or what?" Hae Lana murmured.

"It-it's directly ahead."

My body went cold. "The branches are in the way. I can't see it."

"They sure are. Can the Bolra hear us?" Hae Lana whispered.

"H-hear us? Unknown. According to the fig, the creature has stopped chewing."

I winced. "Is it in the same spot?"

"Na-no, it's moving to our left."

Hae Lana frowned. "Is it climbing or walking?"

"Ah, unknown."

Hae Lana glanced up. "These creatures scare me. They attack from above, to our left, our right or from behind us."

My adrenaline started pumping. "Fire at will."

Ahead, in the near distance, the six-inch-in-diameter head of a white worm popped out of the dirt. It hissed.

Hae Lana fired. The invertebrate ducked and dropped beneath the soil. "Missed. Damn, that thing is quick."

I flinched. "Soaa, can the Bolra hear us?"

"Un-unknown. However, adjacent wimba are complaining about our loud footsteps and booming voices. They say that Teog's will hear them, come this way, then hunt us."

Hae Lana winced.

I sent Hae Lana, M4 and Soaa text, 3D holographic memos, and voicemails with my lenses. While a distant chirping became louder, I remarked, "Anybody, did you receive my recent messages?"

Hae Lana shook her head.

"Ah, no," Soaa commented.

"I did not," M4 replied,

"M-Four, Soaa and Hae Lana, let's use hand signals from now on to communicate. Also, walk softly. Otherwise the Teog will hear us."

"I-I'll use them, but our body odors work better."

I paused, wondering how they would work better. Our group trekked. In the near distance, behind dangling vines, something whirred. I raised my hand, then spread out two of fingers, spelling out a comment. What is making that noise?

To my right, M4 drew a circle in the air with her finger, indicating that she didn't know.

On my left, Hae Lana drew another.

Ahead, leaves blocked my view of Soaa's hands.

My stomach muscles tightened. Above us, hidden in the gloom, canaries chirped three times.

Ahead, Soaa brushed the leaves aside, and spread her fingers apart. Those aren't canaries. Kapoks are squeezing leaves, telling each other that a Teog is crawling over their branches, coming this way.

I blenched. Twenty feet above Soaa, the Teog stopped. It was hard to see because it was the same color as the surrounding leaves.

CHAPTER TWENTY-SIX

I pointed at the beast. Soaa bent her fingers, saying that she noticed it. Within seconds, this new friend said we should move on. Otherwise, the predator would probably strike.

Chills raced up my spine. Our crew slogged on.

When our group climbed over another small hill, the eighth we had encountered, Soaa drew five parallel lines in the air. Four seconds ago, the Teog killed a Toomu, a primate, and ate it. We're safe for the time being because it isn't hungry.

I exhaled, releasing tension.

"Soaa, are you sure? Teog's are tricky," Hae Lana remarked.

"Ya-yes, I am sure."

"I don't believe it. If this predator sneaks up on us, I'm ready."

I glared at Hae Lana. "You should be more alert."

She clenched her teeth. "I'm alert. Everybody else should do the same."

My back muscles tensed up. "We must find Doland and Ze Ma."

Soaa called out for Ze Ma.

"She's probably dead," Hae Lana spat.

"Hae Lana, your statement is premature," M4 said.

"How would you know? It's time to face facts."

I stopped their argument. "Hae Lana, everybody, let's keep looking."

Hae Lana paused, her brow tight. Everybody resumed the search.

After two hours, M4 said, "There is blood on this shiringa's branch. According to my MAW's DNA probe, it belongs to Doland."

I flinched. "He might be wounded. Let's see if we can find him."

"A Teog probably attacked and ate him," Hae Lana blurted.

Chills ran up my spine.

"It-it's possible. But until we find him or his body, it's hard to know," Soaa offered.

Soon after passing bromeliads M4 picked up a severed fingertip. "According to my MAW's DNA probe, this is Doland's."

"An Teog ate him," Hae Lana exclaimed. "I told you so. Everybody should listen to me."

"A Teog or a Bolra left this. Several computer models indicate that this is a warning. The beast wants us to leave its territory."

Hae Lana shook her head. "How would any computer model know that?"

I tried to reassure Hae Lana. "It's important that we find Ze Ma and Doland. However, since our group hasn't found any trace of them, let's return to Homad, get others to join us and try again."

Hae Lana glared at me.

Soaa remarked, "Ye-yes, let's return, then try again." All of us departed.

At dusk, we halted at the edge of a clearing that was twenty-foot in diameter. "Let's camp here for the night," I said.

M4 said she would stand guard the entire evening. Minutes after crawling inside my dome, I dozed off.

Ahead, a tank raced toward me, its gun blasting.

I woke up, covered in sweat, then crawled out of my dome.

"Judging by that look on your face, something scared you," M4 said.

I mentioned the nightmare.

"You've had many of these. It might be a symbol, a way for your mind to help you solve a problem."

"Maybe. I wish they would go away." I went inside the dome and dozed off.

CHAPTER TWENTY-SEVEN

A t dawn our group resumed the journey. Behind us, in the distance, birds whistled.

I blenched. "Soaa, are those canaries?"

"A-according to adjacent creepers, they are."

"Why are they singing? It's a beautiful song," M4 said.

"The-the creepers are saying that male canaries are trying to attract a mate."

Hae Lana shrugged. "Who cares?"

"It's important to keep track of our surroundings," I replied. "Also, AF hasn't repaired any of my lenses' tools."

Hae Lana sighed. "Hasn't? Mine failed, too. I hate it."

"My MAW's screen and its holographic displays are filled with random useless dots. At this point I'm not sure why they're malfunctioning."

I winced.

Hae Lana glowered. "More problems. Shit. And this part of the jungle is just as thick, hard to hike through, as other areas. Son of a bitch." She swatted her wrist. "These tiny flies or whatever they're called are sucking my blood."

I glanced down, noticed a fly on my thumb. I blinked, surprised that the annoying pest was there and pushed it off.

We entered Homad and sat. Ze Ma rushed out of a dome. "You made it."

"Ze Ma, I thought you were dead," Hae Lana said, surprised.

"You made it back. How did you do it?" I asked.

She flinched. "When we were about three hundred yards from Homad, several kapoks told each other that a Teog was close by. Then they pointed out that it was eighty yards behind us, rushing in our direction. I told Doland about it. We hiked straight ahead, the only path that wasn't obstructed by thorn trees. Soon both of us entered thick mist and I lost track of him. I called out his name, but he didn't respond. A few strangler figs told me that if I turned right, there was a narrow path between lupunas. According to the lupunas, if I followed that path, wimba that were close to it would help me reach Homad."

I winced. "And you never heard from Doland again?"

"No."

Hae Lana glowered. "You should have called out his name."

Ze Ma winced. "Several lupunas told me to hike softly. If I didn't a Bolra or Teog would have heard the sound and come after me."

Hae Lana frowned. "Did you make up this story about the lupunas?"

Ze Ma blenched. "No."

I stood in front of Ze Ma and faced Hae Lana. "Don't give her a hard time."

She glared at me. "She needs to hear this. She needs to take responsibility for her actions."

My stomach muscles tightened. "She is lucky to be alive."

Hae Lana shook her head. "You don't know that for sure. If she tried harder, she might have found Doland and helped him reach Homad."

Soaa interrupted our argument. "A-a Teog has arrived. It's eighty feet behind me, hiding behind kapoks."

Hae Lana glanced over her shoulder. "I don't see it."

"It-it's there."

Hae Lana glowered. "I should kill the beast, before it

strikes."

I blinked, surprised. "Stay here. That area is too dark. It would kill you before you have a chance to defend yourself."

Hae Lana raised her fist. "Defend myself? Are you kidding? I'll put bullet holes in its head before it knows what's going on."

"That's an order. Stay here."

This colleague glared at me. "If you say so, sir."

"We we're low on food, need to collect more mushrooms," Soaa remarked.

"Adam, Croll and I can gun down any Teog easily. We should do it before it does the same to us," Hae Lana declared.

My jaw muscles tightened. "It's time to collect more mushrooms. Hae Lana, you, M-Four, and Soaa will accompany me."

Hae Lana's eyes shifted back and forth. "But-but."

I pointed at her. "No back talk. Let's go. It will be darker in a few hours."

Hae Lana sighed and our group set off.

CHAPTER TWENTY-EIGHT

Within minutes, we pushed aside branches. On my right, Soaa commented, "Ac- according to these wimba, there are edible mushrooms five hundred yards ahead of us."

Behind her, Hae Lana said, "This area is hard to hike through. Soaa, isn't there any easier path?"

"The-the others are worse."

Lasers shot out of my RFL, sliced off branches and I stepped forward.

"La-last night I dreamed that after struggling for eight months, I learned how to interpret four hundred more lupunas' signals, an amazing feat."

"Congratulations."

"We should pay attention to our surroundings, not talk about dreams," Hae Lana commented.

I glared at Hae Lana. "Let her talk. The dreams could be more important than you think."

"More important than fighting off a Teog? Are you shitting me?"

My neck muscles tightened. "No, I'm not."

Hae Lana sighed. "If you say so."

Our crew halted at the mushroom patch. Several members picked some, and tossed them in their mouths. Bags popped out of their belts and the bags expanded. Everybody flung the fungi into them.

"Last night I dreamed that I taught classes on Laasp, rarely left it," Hae Lana said.

145

"Did you want to stay on Laasp?" I asked.

"No. Teaching aboard a starship or any kind of spacecraft was far more exciting."

I nodded.

We left the patch. Ahead, to our right, behind Pallas, a soft clicking, barely audible, grew louder. I flinched. "There isn't enough light to see what is making that noise."

"Ac-according to a vine, three butterflies are mating."

I exhaled, releasing tension.

Our group entered Homad. The floating bags touched down on tables, then opened. Everybody but M4 sat and ate.

"Last night, I dreamed that En Ana and I had a child, a boy," Xa Om said.

Ze Ma stared at him sharply. "You told me you didn't like her."

"I never did. It was a nightmare."

"Two nights ago, I dreamed that you, Mother, died," Wo Ra shared.

"That's horrible."

"It was," Wo Ra blurted. "It was almost as real as being awake."

Ze Ma sighed, then caressed her daughter's cheek. "My child, please don't talk like this. You're young, ready for a full life."

Wo Ra cringed. "Mother, what about you? Any dreams?"

She sighed. "Four nights ago, Xa Om and I had a son, not a daughter. It was a realistic nightmare. I'm glad that he married me, and we had you." She grabbed her daughter's hand and squeezed it.

Browna frowned. "This is thought-provoking. Everybody, including me, is dreaming a lot."

I asked Dr. Browna about her dreams.

"In mine, I became an ambulance driver, not a doctor, and ended up treating patients in the Fot War."

I blinked, surprised. "Why did you become a doctor?"

She flinched. "It was my mother's idea. Although the idea of getting into medical school and graduating felt like an impossible goal, she advised me to do it. I told her every course was tough. She pointed out that doctors are highly respected. Anyway, a few months later, I applied to five medical schools. One accepted me. I was shocked that they did. A few weeks after school started, I found out that I loved the challenge, much to my surprise."

"In some cases challenges are helpful," I told her.

Browna nodded. "Some are."

M4 remarked in a monotone, "The volcanic dust has stopped plummeting."

"That's good news," I said. "By the way, it's late, time to bed down for the night."

At sun up, Ze Ma left dome B and sat at a table.

"Did you sleep well?" I asked.

She flinched. "According to three kapoks, a Bolra has arrived."

A chill ran up my spine. I glanced to the right, left, ahead and behind me, but only noticed the jungle. "Where is it?"

"Sixty yards to your right, hiding behind strangler figs."

I looked in that direction. "I can't see it."

"It's there."

The ground shook. I winced. "Earthquake."

M4 stepped out of dome E. "Pressure is building up inside the volcano. It will explode in approximately five days, two hours and three minutes. At that point, lava will flow this way. A safer location is half a mile from the originator, on Mt. Teil's east slope."

I blenched. "Are there any edible roots or palatable

mushrooms on its east slope?"

"Absolutely not. The closest edible roots are one point two miles north of the slope, three fourths of a mile from the lava flow."

I imagined the lava sweeping us away. "M-Four, does Dr. Croll know of a safe area that is close to the roots, a location where Fane can land?"

Croll stepped out of dome F. "I heard that. We'll have to touch down next to the originator."

Hae Lana rushed out of dome G. "M-Four, are you sure about the volcano exploding?"

"Eighty-five percent sure."

Hae Lana shook her head. "That means there is a fifteen percent chance that you are wrong. And since we're surrounded by trees that might be blocking your probes, your estimation could be one hundred percent off."

"One hundred percent is extreme. My MAW probed the volcano sixteen times in the last eleven hours."

Hae Lana glowered. "I don't believe it. We should stay here."

My stomach muscles tightened. "We're leaving in thirty minutes."

Hae Lana glared at me, then grumbled incoherently.

Our domes moved together, then changed into a bullet shape—Fane's new form—and rose. Soon our vessel veered port. When our craft was sixty feet from the originator, a huge flock of winged creatures with a ten-foot wingspan, took off.

"These birds or whatever they are, are blocking our descent," Hae Lana exclaimed.

I flinched. "Hold on. It's time to go around them."

"Damn, their beaks are razor sharp."

Fane swerved port, dropped, then touched down. Within seconds, the hull separated into eighteen domes, a place M4 called New Homad. I stepped out of one and looked up. Above me, forty of the winged creatures were circling.

On my left, Hae Lana, looked up at the sky. "What are they looking for?"

To my right, M4 said, "At this point, unknown."

"They look ominous," Croll remarked.

Without warning, three dropped.

"They're attacking," Hae Lana hollered. Everybody fired. Our surroundings fragmented, then faded.

CHAPTER TWENTY-NINE

Much to my surprise, M4, Hae Lana, and I were standing on the deck of a sixty-foot-long boat that resembled a whale. As it went over a wave, Hae Lana glowered. "We're in the middle of an ocean. How did we get here?"

"Hard to say," I replied.

M4 noted our companions' absence. "Xa Om, Wo Ra, Ze Ma, Soaa, and Dr. Croll aren't with us."

I nodded. To my right, in the near distance, a six-foot-tall chrome humanoid robot, one of five, walked across the deck, then pointed at me. "Ah en." My earplugs translated, "You appeared out of nowhere a moment ago. Who sent you here?"

I paused, dumbfounded. "Who? I don't know. What is your name?" My earplugs offered a translation in this robot's language, Le Op.

"Prov Nine. What are yours?"

I answered.

"Unfamiliar monikers," Prov-9 said. Orlan, a Maen, the leader of a group of scientists who created us forty years ago, might have sent you. However, I'm not sure how or why he did."

My earplugs updated my hippocampus. Now I understood everything Prov-9 said and could speak to him in Le Op.

On my left, Hae Lana frowned. "Who are the Maen?"

"A race of beings," explained Prov-9.

"Where are the Maen?" I asked.

Prov-9 answered in a monotone. "Sixteen years ago or four

150

summers after they created all eighteen of us—the Denb—every Maen died, killed by a virus."

"Nine, why are you along with every Denb aboard this ship, sailing across an ocean?" M4 said.

"Fourteen years ago, two oceans—we call Naet and Cora—rose and covered all seven islands on this planet, one called Amb."

I winced. "Where did all the water come from?"

"Melted polar icecaps."

Hae Lana glowered. "Who built this ship?"

"We, the Denb, did."

"What is its name?" I asked.

"The Wond."

Hae Lana pointed to the left. "A huge fish is coming this way. Shit."

I glanced the direction she had pointed at and noticed a six-foot-high dorsal fin that made me flinch.

"A Slen is usually forty glips long," Prov-9 informed us.

According to my lens, a glip is equal to one foot. I winced. "Will the Slen attack us?"

"By all means," said Prov-9. The fish rammed the boat, then swam away.

Hae Lana cringed. "Is it trying to sink the Wond?"

"No doubt about it." The android yanked a two-inch long pistol off its chest and the weapon clicked.

It surprised me. "Does your gun work?"

"Of course. It shot molecular cutters into the Slen's back."

Hae Lana glowered. "Will the cutter's kill it?"

"It takes about forty shots to do that." The vertebrate's dorsal fin moved to the left and started circling the boat.

"Is it closing in?" M4 asked?

"No doubt about it," Prov-9 said.

About two hundred yards off the bow, eight fins, all seven feet high came out of the water.

Hae Lana winced, then pointed at them. "More Slens have arrived."

Prov-9 nodded. "True."

Hae Lana, M4 and I raised our arms, ready to fire.

Nine pointed at them. "Why did you lift those?"

I told the android about our weapons.

"A curious sight," Prov-9 commented.

To the android's right, its five other shipmates, bronze androids, yanked guns off their chests. The Slen's began circling.

"I don't know how much more of this I can take," Hae Lana blurted.

Chills ran up my spine. "Hold your fire until they're closer."

"A couple of well-aimed shots would scare them off," Hae Lana snapped.

I shook my head. "Wait until I give the order." One raised its snout out of the water and water dripped off its four-inch high teeth.

Hae Lana winced. "They could bite you in half in one second."

My adrenaline pumped harder. Much to my surprise, the carnivore dropped into the water. Within seconds, these predators veered to the left and swam away.

"Why did they leave?" M4 asked.

Prov-9 looked at M4. "A well evaluated point. Normally, they would close in, then ram our boat several times. When it tipped over, they would maul us."

"Have you seen them tip a boat over and attack?" I asked, curious.

"Of course."

"More details would help," said M4.

"The event took place two years ago. It was a useless effort because the Denb are inedible. However, my estimation is that the Slen do this for pleasure."

Hae Lana glowered. "They're hideous predators. I want to kill as many as possible."

Thirty minutes later, twenty yards from us, fifteen Slen fins rose out of surf and moved toward the boat.

"Trouble. Fuckers," Hae Lana spat.

When they were several feet away, I yelled, "Fire!"

Beams hit the fish. They rammed their snouts against the hull. Hae Lana, M4, Prov-9, several other Denb and I stumbled, then landed on the deck.

"We don't have a chance. Shit," Hae Lana yelled.

"Two probability graphs indicate we have a twenty-one percent chance," M4 said.

As the Slen banged their snouts against the hull, all of us jumped up and sprayed the predators with laser beams and ammo.

One Slen growled. *Yooan.*

"A repulsive noise," exclaimed Hae Lana.

I flinched while more bullets struck their fins and heads.

"What does it take to scare them off?"

M4 quickly glanced at her. "Intriguing statement."

One Denb tripped and fell overboard.

"Shit," yelled Hae Lana. She raced over and stuck out her hand, trying to grab the robot. The Denb seized her fingers as a Slen bit off the robot's right leg. Hae Lana pulled the android onto the deck. All the predators backed away and submerged.

I flinched. "Where did they go?"

"Hard to tell. Keep a sharp lookout," Prov-9 said.

The maimed robot crawled across the deck.

Hae Lana frowned. "Nine, can you repair your associate's leg?"

"Maybe. We'll tie pieces of wood to Prov-sixteen's hip. With some luck and practice my shipmate can hobble around."

Chills ran up my spine. In my imagination, the Slen ripped my body apart.

"Two quantum probability graphs indicate that there is a sixty percent chance that Prov-sixteen can move around slowly with its homemade crutch," said M4.

Hae Lana glowered.

Twenty minutes later, a flock of ten-feet-long winged reptiles with two-foot-long beaks and leathery skin arrived. A few screeched. *Eeeto.*

"They're hideous and they smell like shit," Hae Lana observed.

I flinched. "Yes."

"Their bodies are covered by tiny worms," M4 noted.

"Yuck," commented Hae Lana.

"Those are called Winje," Prov-9 told us.

Three of them swooped down. Prov-9, the bronze robots, M4, Hae Lana, and I sprayed them with ammo.

Eeeto. One reached down with its claws, then grabbed Prov-9's arm. All of us fired. *Eeeto.* It rose, flapping hard as drool slid off both jaws. The Winje dropped Prov-9 and the robot landed on the deck, feet first. At the same time, slimy five-foot-long worms fell off the creature. Soon they crawled toward M4. Laser beams from our weapons struck the invertebrates. They hissed. *Ssssah.*

"Those worms are ugly," shouted Hae Lana.

My stomach muscles tightened. One wrapped itself around M4's foot. At the same time, it opened its jaws and bit her ankle.

"It won't let go," Hae Lana spat.

A blade popped out of M4's wrist. "That is correct." She reached down and sliced the worm's head off. The body part dropped onto the deck, then rolled across it.

More slithered toward Hae Lana. Ammo struck them.

Sssssah. Without warning, the invertebrates halted.

A few minutes later Prov-9 announced, "They're dead."

Fifteen feet above our group, the creatures flapped harder. We fired at them. *Eeeeto*. They defecated on the deck, then turned, flew away, and stopped.

I winced. "Nine, will they come back?"

"Perhaps."

I looked at M4 and Hae Lana. "If they come any closer, shoot to kill."

"I hate them," said Hae Lana.

While chills ran up my spine, the winged creatures started circling the boat.

"Go away," yelled Hae Lana.

M4 pointed at them. "Your effort to scare them off failed."

Hae Lana glared at the robot. "Obviously. Stop giving me a hard time."

M4 paused with a blank expression on her face.

Much to my surprise, the reptiles took off.

Hae Lana sighed. "Good riddance."

I turned to Prov-9. "Will they come back?"

"If they're hungry, chances are that they will. If we're lucky, they will locate grig and ignore us."

According to my lenses, grig were fish.

It's time to clean," Prov-9 announced. If we don't shove the droppings into the sea, they will attract thousands of yaolos."

Bronze Provos climbed out of an open hatch, mops in hand, then used them to shove the droppings into rising surf.

According to my lenses, yaolos were two-foot-long winged reptiles, a species that spit lethal venom.

"I'm glad they're doing that. The stench is getting worse," Hae Lana exclaimed.

Prov-9 pointed at me. "Would you and your friends like something to eat?"

I said we would. Provo-9 called out, asking another Provo for a meal. Soon a robot dashed out of an open hatch and gave Hae Lana and I a bowl filled with grubs.

Hae Lana winced. "These are edible?"

"They are a delicacy."

"A scan indicates they're filled with Vitamin C and protein," M4 added.

Hae Lana grabbed a few, stuffed them in her mouth and chewed.

My stomach muscles tightened. "What do they taste like?"

She glowered. "Greasy potatoes."

I flinched, seized a couple, tossed them in my mouth and munched.

Hae Lana frowned. "Commander, judging by that look on your face, you don't like them."

I sighed. "They're an acquired taste. However, since I'm hungry, eating them is important." My lenses sent neutrinos into Nine's hippocampus. Much to my surprise, the particles returned.

One hundred and eighty years ago, in the year fifteen, Hargo invented the gas-powered engine. Two summers later, Hargo and several Maen placed these engines on boats. Within three winters, two hundred boats with these types of engines, transported passengers, food, spices and other materials between all seven of Amb's islands.

In the year twenty-four, Lecto built the first airplane. Thirty-four summers later, Denb created a virus, one designed to wipe out a humanoid group called the Opers. However, the virus — a pathogen he called Unre — began spreading uncontrollably — a shocking and unplanned event.

I winced.

Hae Lana frowned. "Adam, judging by that expression on your face, something is bothering you. Is it the food?"

I told her about Amb's past.

"That's disgusting. The Denb should have planned better."

"That is true. We should have," Prov-9 said.

Several hours later, at sunset, my head started throbbing.

Prov-9 noticed my headache. "You have been exposed to Unre. You will be dead within two weeks."

I winced. "Are there any cures?"

"Under no circumstances."

"This is horrible. My head is throbbing, too," Hae Lana exclaimed.

"I don't know much about your race, but it's sad that both of you won't ever explore our vast beautiful oceans."

Then the Provs and everything else vanished.

CHAPTER THIRTY

Ahead, in the near distance, M4, Soaa, Wo Ra, Ze Ma and Hae Lana walked toward huge trees, ones made of crystal.

"Hae Lana, my headache is gone," I said.

She offered a faint grin. "So is mine."

To my left, Croll frowned. "Adam, a few seconds ago, when I was in Homad, M-Four, Hae Lana, and you vanished. I asked Xa Om, Wo Ra, Ze Ma, and Soaa what happened to all three of you. All four told me they didn't know. Where did all three of you go?"

I blinked, caught off guard by his question, then answered.

Croll flinched. "That's peculiar. I don't buy it."

I bit my lip, bothered by his inability to accept my explanation.

"On the other hand, I have no idea how we ended up in this freakish location."

Hae Lana defended me. "Adam's response is correct."

Croll winced. "M-Four, was Adam's response accurate?"

"Affirmative."

Croll glowered. "Odd. Like I said, how did we end up here?"

My jaw muscles tightened. "I wish I knew. Unfortunately my lenses are partly filled with random, useless dashes."

"These trees called themselves the Holden," Wo Ra said.

Hae Lana glared at her. "Did you make that up?"

"I did not."

Hae Lana shook her head. "It sounds like a fairy tale."

Ze Ma ignored Hae Lana. "Wo Ra, what else did the Holden say?"

"That we have invaded the Scora's territory."

Hae Lana glowered. "Who are the Scora?"

"The Holden did not say," Wo Ra replied.

Hae Lana shook her head. "There aren't any Scora. The Holden are just a bunch of dumb trees. They don't talk."

"Two Holden told me that sixteen Scora will arrive soon. The Scora are angry, do not like invaders."

"I don't want to fight, yet will do so if necessary," commented Xa Om.

"We should talk to them, point . . . point out that our group is peaceful," advised Ze Ma.

Minutes later, three four-feet-long insects, a species with fly like heads and thoraxes that were covered by triangular plates rushed out from behind several trees.

I winced, shocked by their appearance, then raised my arm, ready to fire. "Don't shoot until I give the order."

Hae Lana raised her arm and pointed it at them. "Are those Scora?"

"According to a Holden, they are," Wo Ra replied.

Hae Lana glowered. "They're mouths are lined with huge teeth."

I flinched. "Why are they making that scratching noise?"

"They are talking to each other," Wo Ra informed us.

"Are you kidding?" Hae Lana blurted. "It sounds meaningless."

"I am not kidding."

Soaa blenched.

Chills ran up my spine. "What are they saying?

"The biggest, who calls himself Cles, told me we are intruders," Wo Ra commented.

"Tell him we ended up here by accident and don't know

where to go," Ze Ma said.

"Cles' friend, Anig, told him that you are lying. Anig said our group's real goal is to kill them and take over this territory," remarked Wo Ra.

My mind sped up, trying to come up with a solution. "Wo Ra, is there anything you can say or do that would convince them that we're peaceful, won't hurt them or take over this area?"

Wo Ra made squeaky noises with her mouth.

Croll flinched but didn't say anything.

Hae Lana frowned. "Wo Ra why are you making those odd sounds?"

"I repeated Adam's statement. Hopefully Cles will listen and leave us alone."

Hae Lana glowered. "The idea that you can communicate with them is foolish."

Cles rubbed his jaws together.

"Cles said if we leave now and head for the Ble grasslands, most of the Scora will not kill us," commented Wo Ra.

I talked to Wo Ra without taking my gaze off the Scora. "Where is the Ble and how far away is it?"

"It is due south, about forty-two groogs from here."

Hae Lana sighed. "What is a groog?"

Wo Ra hissed three times.

Soaa cringed.

Hae Lana's brow tightened. "Are you talking to Cles? It's a freakish noise."

"Yes. He said that our group can reach Ble in eight hours. However, we'll have to cross the Uig's territory."

I flinched. "What or who are the Uig?"

Wo Ra made a puffing noise with her mouth.

Cles' jaw twitched.

"I did not understand Cles' answer."

Hae Lana's mouth twisted. "Just great. We're bound for an

unknown destination and have to deal with freakish creatures, a species that might kill or ignore us."

"Let's go," I said.

Huge insects, all similar to Cles arrived.

Ze Ma pointed at them. "Wo Ra, are they going to slaughter us?"

She made five scratching noises with her mouth. Two were a second long, the rest were five seconds in length.

Hae Lana sighed.

Croll shrugged.

Soaa cringed.

"Hae Lana be patient," I said.

"I am."

"Cles told me that we should walk slowly. Do not jerk our arms or legs. If we do, many Scora will strike because they feel threatened by sudden movement," Wo Ra said.

Hae Lana groaned.

"Cles isn't responding to my body odor," Soaa remarked.

"Hae Lana, everybody pay attention to Wo Ra's directions," I said.

Hae Lana glared at me. "What the hell do you think I'm doing, sir?"

My stomach muscles tightened. Our small group turned and departed. Ahead, a wall of Scora crawled aside. One remained, its jaws quivering.

Xa Om pointed at it. "What is this creature saying?"

"If we step on its foot, he will eat one of us," Wo Ra translated.

Xa Om flinched. Every member of our group hiked around this beast, our feet inches from his. Ahead, fourteen more of them blocked our way.

I blenched. "Wo Ra, are they going to move aside?"

She winced. "Maybe."

Much to my surprise, they spread apart.

Xa Om whispered, "This is horrible. They're grinding their teeth, ready to tear us apart."

"The-they're ignoring my body odor, a scent that tells them we're not going to hurt them," Soaa commented.

"Using your body odor to do that is dumb," said Hae Lana. Soaa flinched.

My body went cold. "Let's keep going."

One of the creatures made a soft whooping noise with its mouth.

"One of them told me that our entire group must quit staring at them. If we do not, they will rip our arms off and eat us," said Wo Ra,

"Shit. Shit. Shit," Hae Lana muttered.

Croll sighed.

Ze Ma shuddered. "There are so many of them."

Xa Om gasped. "They smell like death."

"Xa Om, everybody, don't make so much noise," I said.

One Scora stuck out its leg and dragged it over Ze Ma's hip. She bit her lip.

"Mom, do not push the leg off. If you do, the other Scora will strike," said Wo Ra.

Ze Ma nodded, her teeth clenched.

"If we get out of here alive, I'll have nightmares about this for years," Hae Lana murmured.

I clenched my teeth, horrified.

CHAPTER THIRTY-ONE

Ahead, five Scora hopped off trees, and ended up on the ground.

"They're blocking our route. Son of a bitch," exclaimed Hae Lana.

I winced. "Let's go around them."

A Scora jumped on Ze Ma's stomach, crawled down it, and halted, its legs twitching.

She bit her lip. The insect raced down her leg, injected something into it with a thorax-mounted stinger.

This new friend began trembling. The invertebrate crawled onto the ground.

"Mom, does the sting hurt?" asked Wo Ra.

"Yes, a lot. The pain is getting worse."

Wo Ra put her arm around her and they continued on.

Hae Lana glowered. "Just great. With our luck she'll be dead soon."

"Hae Lana, help her, quit complaining," I said.

My colleague glared at me, then put her arm around Ze Ma and all of us kept going. Soon Ze Ma's head drooped forward.

"Mom, do not fall asleep or you might not wake up," said Wo Ra.

Ze Ma's head jerked upward, an inch, then dropped.

Hae Lana sighed. "Ze Ma, wake up." My colleague shook Ze Ma's shoulder.

I winced. "Wo Ra and Hae Lana, keep trying."

"I'm doing my best," snapped Hae Lana.

Ze Ma's body went limp and her feet started dragging.

Hae Lana sighed. "It's a good thing that she is easy to carry."

"Mom, can you hear me?"

Wo Ra's mother didn't respond.

Croll looked at Ze Ma closer. "Oh no."

Chills ran up my spine.

"Her situation looks bad. Let's hope she will survive," said Hae Lana. She nodded and pointed ahead of us. "More trouble."

A small group of Scora raced toward us. One jumped up, landed on Hae Lana's hand, bit off her tiny finger then hopped off.

My colleague winced. "Damn it to hell, that hurts."

I reached down. A nozzle popped out of my sleeve and it sprayed her hand. "The bleeding will stop in two seconds."

Hae Lana bit her lip. "The pain."

Our group came upon two half eaten rabbit corpses. Eight Scora ripped flesh off them.

Xa Om cringed. "What a ghastly sight."

I winced. "Let's go around them."

"Very well," exclaimed Xa Om.

Our group veered to the left, stepped over ribs, hiked on and went between piled up clavicles.

Xa Om couldn't stop staring at the massacre. "Gro-grotesque."

Ahead about twenty orange flies swooped down, came to rest on skulls, and crawled over them. Soon the insects spit on the jaws.

I cringed.

Hae Lana coughed. "The stench is unbearable." She vomited.

I exhaled, trying to calm down. "Breathe through your mouth."

Hae Lana choked. "Let's hope that works."

Our group walked between femurs and broken pelvis bones.

Xa Om flinched. "I just stepped on an eyeball."

Hae Lana recoiled.

Minutes later, we came upon a stream, then hiked through it.

"Keep up the pace," I told the crew. We reached the opposite shore, then passed huge crystal bushes.

"These plants look like they're made of quartz and dried saliva," said Xa Om.

Hae Lana glowered. "Are you kidding me?"

"The best word I can think of is no."

My colleague glared at him, then looked straight ahead with an irritated expression on her face.

Soon our crew slogged over a hill.

Hae Lana groaned. "According to my lenses, Ze Ma is dead, passed away two minutes ago."

Xa Om paused, his teeth clenched. "I loved her."

Wo Ra started trembling.

I flinched. "Let's bury her here." Tiny excavators, equipment that was the same size as a piece of dust popped out of Hae Lana's sleeve and mine. Within seconds, these tools expanded, then dug.

Within minutes, the excavators tossed the last pile of dirt on the grave. Hae Lana sighed. "That was horrible. Adam, you should have known this would happen."

I winced. "That's impossible."

Xa Om wailed, then hugged Wo Ra.

Soaa wiped tears off her cheek.

Croll paused, then choked up.

Hae Lana shook her head. "Adam, you upset Xa Om and

Wo Ra."

I blurted, "Knock it off. We have to find a safe area. Your help is needed to achieve that goal."

Hae Lana glared at me. "Yes sir." Our group tramped on.

To my left, Xa Om and Wo Ra began trembling.

Chills ran up my spine. "She was a great friend," I told them.

Both of them frowned and lowered their heads. Without warning, both halted and hid their faces with both hands.

Hae Lana and I stopped. I bit my lip, knowing my last statement was the kindest comment I could say.

Xa Om and Wo Ra pulled their hands away, then hiked. Much to my surprise, both hummed.

I blinked, caught off guard. Were they singing a particular song?

At dusk, our troop came upon the edge of a grass plain. "Let's camp here for the night," I said.

On my right, Croll nodded.

Next to him, Xa Om sighed. "A g-good idea."

To my left, M4 said, "It's time to rest."

"Xa Om, what was the name of that song you were humming?" I asked.

His shoulders drooped. "Ov Ort."

Hae Lana frowned. "What does that mean?"

Xa Om raised a trembling hand, then examined it. "It honors the great deeds and kinds words of dead loved ones."

Hae Lana sat, her lips contorted. "My mother, father, and brother passed away years ago."

"I'm sorry to hear it," said Xa Om.

Hae Lana's brow tightened. "I don't like to think about it because it makes me sad. It's better to focus on the future."

I blinked, caught off guard by Hae Lana's comment. "Hae Lana, you've never talked about it before."

She glanced at the sky with a sad expression on her face. "It's better that way."

Xa Om hummed.

M4 listened with a blank expression on her face.

"Xa Om, what is the name of that song?" I asked.

"Ob on."

"Does it mention the dead?"

"No, it's about the end of the day, when much hard work is finished."

"The tune sounds sad."

"It d-does." Soaa examined her shaking hand.

"Soaa, you look upset."

"I-I am."

In the near distance, a chirping became louder.

"What is making that sound?" blurted Hae Lana.

"According to the bushes, they are harmless insects called Oled," replied Wo Ra.

Hae Lana glowered. "Are you sure?"

"Not totally."

Hae Lana frowned. "With our luck, they will attack, rip off our skin and eat us."

My stomach muscles tightened. "Hae Lana, be patient. Don't jump to conclusions."

She clenched her fist. "Shoot first, then ask questions later. That's my motto. Otherwise you'll end up dead."

"Don't shoot until I give the order," I announced.

She clenched her teeth. "Yes sir. But if they strike and kill anybody, it's your fault, not mine."

My stomach muscles tightened. "I'll take that responsibility."

My colleague sighed. "Commander Adam, you're an idealist. You should be more cautious, like me. In a kill or be killed universe, realists like me will thrive. Idealists like you will perish."

I bit my lip, irritated. "You didn't talk like this when we were on Laasp or Yerak."

She glared at me. "I've learned a lot since then."

I bit my lip, annoyed. "Alright, you've had your say. Now pay attention and do what I say."

Her brow tightened. "What a mess, what a fucking mess we're in."

Ahead, far away, eight creatures, barely visible in tall grass, dashed toward us. I flinched, then pointed at them. "Something is coming."

"Shit. My lenses can't ID them. AF hasn't repaired them," said Hae Lana.

"According to the grass, the creatures call themselves the Uig," commented Wo Ra.

"You made that up."

"I did not."

"Hae Lana, your criticism is based on fear, not fact," Xa Om remarked.

"Xa Om, can you hear yourself? Your comment is based on fantasy. Mine is based on truth."

I bit my lip, annoyed by my colleague's cynical attitude. "Hae Lana, Wo Ra is perceptive. Pay attention to her comments."

She glared at me. "Yes sir." This colleague along with everybody else raised their arms, ready to fire.

I turned right. Far away, two ten-foot-long arachnids — an ebony species with huge claws crawled over grass — were heading our way.

Hae Lana pointed at them. "They're covered by mucus."

I flinched. Within seconds, both creatures started circling us. On top of their heads, a stinger lurched forward and stopped.

"We should kill them before they attack," Hae Lana called out.

I winced. "Wait until they're closer."

Hae Lana coughed. "They smell like stomach bile."

Both creatures squealed. *Yeeap.*

"What a sickening noise," announced Xa Om.

Chills ran up my spine.

Wo Ra flinched.

Soaa cringed.

The predators scampered toward us, their claws open. Laser beams struck them. *Yeeeaaap.*

"Got one," yelled Hae Lana.

"My first shot struck one's leg," said M4.

Both creatures halted. At the same time their stingers sprayed a cloud of droplets.

"I can't see," Hae Lana hollered. "That mist has blinded me."

I ducked. While droplets trickled down my chest, more ammo struck both creatures. They halted, eight feet from us.

"My gun is jammed," Xa Om called out.

"Try again," I announced. Laser beams from our weapons struck their legs. *Yeeeap.* They backed away, then stopped thirty feet from our group.

"Hitting them with our ammo or laser beams is tough because they're so far away. Wait until they come closer," I said.

"Why d-don't they charge?" remarked Xa Om.

Chills ran up my spine. "Good question. My best guess is that they'll do that any second." My lenses sent neutrinos into their minds. The particles returned. "According to my last probe, they called themselves the Uig. These predators want to eat us soon."

"Awfuul," remarked Xa Om.

Soaa coughed.

"Aim carefully," said M4.

"My eyes hurt. Opening them is painful. I hate this," said Hae Lana.

I winced. "Keep your eyes closed."

"Damn it. I don't want to die like this."

Faraway, another Uig rushed toward us.

Xa Om said, "Wo Ra, you're shaking like grass," said Xa Om.

"I am scared."

CHAPTER THIRTY-TWO

The third Uig halted between the others.

"What are they doing?" said Xa Om.

I blenched. "Good question." Without warning everything stretched, then disappeared. M4, Wo Ra, and I were standing twenty feet from a group of clowns. All of them yanked out their swords and began dueling.

On my right, Wo Ra said, "Where is Hae Lana and the other crew?"

"Hard to say," I answered.

To my left, M4 said, "Adam, according to my MAW, this group calls themselves the Feof." The tallest sliced his opponent's head off.

I winced. "They don't mess around."

Wo Ra placed both hands over her contact lenses. "I do not want to notice anymore."

The swordsman started dueling with another clown, a stranger who resembled me.

I cringed. "When I was a kid, I admired clowns, thought they were funny."

"Obviously these aren't funny," remarked M4.

Another Feof raced toward me, his sword raised. He shouted. A translation came out of my earplugs — Enemy.

I flinched, then dodged to the left as this stranger sliced a piece of material off my right shoulder pad. Then I spun around. He thrust his blade forward. I stepped aside while my laser beam struck his throat. He screamed and collapsed. Behind me, others hollered. A translation came out — Death to the trespassers. I did an about face.

Laser beams from M4's wrist struck two clown's jaws. One hollered. A translation came out—No . . . Both stumbled and landed face down in dirt. Behind them, three more darted toward her. She and I sprayed them with ammo. Two screamed, took a few steps and dropped to the ground, blood running down their cheeks.

Not far beyond them, two other Feof pointed at us and bellowed. A translation came out of my lenses—You will die soon. Both turned and ran away.

Wo Ra lowered her trembling hands. "They are gone. That is wonderful. Will they return?"

My heart pounded. "Return? Hard to say."

"An aggressive group," commented M4. "Wo Ra, you handled yourself well for someone your age."

"Thank you." She examined her quivering hand.

"Where are we?" I asked M4.

"According to my shoulder-mounted MCIT there are eight thousand, four hundred stars in the sky. Based on that, we are in another universe."

I blinked, astonished. "How did we get here?"

"I might be able to answer that later, when more accurate star maps and coordinates are available. At this point my MCIT is sorting data."

I bit my lip, frustrated. "Let me know when it's available."

M4 nodded.

"The nearby kapoks are sending out messages," said Wo Ra.

I blinked, amazed. "What are they saying?"

"The three of us are outsiders, incapable of talking or listening to them."

"Who is them?" M4 asked.

"The kapoks."

I hesitated, surprised. "Wo Ra, can the Feof talk to the

kapoks?"

"Some can."

"Fascinating," commented M4.

Ahead, sixteen Feof rushed out from behind kapoks, raised their swords, and darted toward us.

I flinched. M4 and I fired.

CHAPTER THIRTY-THREE

Our beams struck them. Eight collapsed. Thirty more darted out from behind the kapoks.

My body went cold.

"There are too many to kill. We're in trouble," said M4.

Everything melted, then vanished. Now I was standing between M4 and Hae Lana. In front of us, about thirty yards away, two five-foot-tall humanoids with oblong heads walked toward our group. These unfamiliar entities with slit-like eyes yanked arrows out of their chest-mounted quivers and placed them on their bows.

Hae Lana raised her arm, ready to fire. "Are they going to shoot us?"

"According to a probability chart, there is sixty percent chance that they will," said M4.

"Damn it, I'm tired, don't want to fight."

My stomach muscles tightened. "Let's hope we can talk to them, avoid a fight."

Hae Lana sighed. "I'm for that. By the way, where is the rest of the crew?"

"Unknown," said M4.

"M-Four, you're cool under pressure."

To our left, behind towering bushes, a thrumming became louder.

Hae Lana frowned. "What's making that creepy noise?"

"Good question," I said.

On our left, three four-foot-long winged creatures with leathery skin and large beaks flew over the bushes, flapping.

M4 pointed at the birds. "They're coming this way."

"Damn it," Hae Lana shouted. "They're making that creepy noise."

Both humanoids raised their bows, fired arrows and a projectile struck one creature's wing. It shrieked. *Oooowea*. Both creatures veered left, flew away and disappeared into thick mist.

The thinner humanoid turned toward us and commented, "Aray."

A translation came out of my earplugs. "Who are you?"

I offered my name.

The humanoid blinked. "Notay."

Another came out. "You are unfamiliar. Why have you come here?"

I answered. My lenses sent this stranger my answer in his language, called Zan.

"Tikanes. Mo ze."

"Cannot translate."

I sighed. "M-Four, can you decipher his last comment? My lenses can't."

"He says his name is Gax. He is a member of the Taon race. Gax says we're in great danger because this area, the Oix jungle is filled Yaan."

"What is a Yaan?"

Gax motioned with his hand.

"Gax says it's the name of the winged creatures, the species they scared off with their arrows."

"A couple of Yaan aren't bone-chilling," Hae Lana blurted.

M4 talked to Gax. "Nolo fala."

Gax nodded.

"Hae Lana, Adam, I just told Gax that."

Hae Lana shrugged. "Why are we in great danger?"

"Lel la ah."

"Gax said that there are millions of Yaan in this area."

I winced. "M-Four, does Gax know if the Yaan will attack us?" My lenses sent neutrinos into this being's hippocampus.

"He said they usually eat rats. However, if these predators can't find any they will slaughter us."

My body went cold.

Hae Lana glowered. "Damn it. M-Four, will they tear you apart?"

"Affirmative."

I blenched. "M-Four, does Gax know how the Taon survive?"

Gax made a swishing noise with his mouth.

"He says it's a constant battle."

Hae Lana shook her head. "Shit, we're in big trouble."

Gax clench his teeth and exhaled. "An on ey."

A translation came out—"There is a solution."

My adrenaline pumped harder. "What is it?"

"Lo on. To on," replied Gax.

My lenses translated. "Set fire to their nests. Because most of the Yaan live close to them, you will destroy the vast majority of these creatures. The rest will leave, then set up their nests in another part of the Cihen Jungle, the one we're in."

"Finding them is tough," Hae Lana blurted. "Gax, M-Four, where are they?"

The Guga, translated our lenses.

"That's a start," I said.

Where is the Guga?" asked Hae Lana.

"Can a."

"M-Four, what is he saying?"

"That he will take us there," I said.

"Adam, how do you understand what he is saying?"

I answered.

"Damn, why won't my mind understand everything he is saying?"

"That will take time," M4 said.

Gax's mouth tightened into a frown. "Ho wi."

"What? I don't understand."

"He said that we have to set fire to the nests when the parents are away," I translated for her.

Hae Lana blinked. "When is that?"

Gax said, "If the father can't locate food for the babies, the mother joins him."

"Na nin," commented M4.

"M-Four asked Gax how often are both away," I informed Hae Lana.

She frowned. "Adam, thanks for the translation. How often are both away?"

"Gax says it's hard to say. Somebody will have to watch the nest, " M4 answered.

Hae Lana scowled.

M4 commented, "Or a."

"My mind has adapted. M-Four said she will watch it."

Gax flinched, then looked at M4. "You are a brave soul."

M4 nodded.

I winced. "Gax, how many of your friends have watched Yaan nests?"

"Five."

"How many survived?"

Gax blenched. "None."

My body went cold.

Thirty minutes later, M4 and I halted behind towering bushes. A Yaan flew overhead. I cringed.

"Stay here and stand guard, Adam. If any Yaan attack me, kill them."

I nodded. She turned into a Yaan.

I blinked, startled. My colleague stepped around the bush, crept toward the nest. I peeked between leaves. She sat next to it. Five Yaan snarled at her.

She hissed at them.

All five opened their beaks.

M4's message scrolled through my lenses. *According to my MAW, all five are suspicious, say they don't recognize my odor.*

I winced, not sure how to respond.

A flame shot out of her claw and engulfed about eighty nests. A huge group of Yaan, about fifty, shrieked as the nests caught on fire. Six raced toward her. Three tore her wings off. Everything turned gray.

CHAPTER THIRTY-FOUR

I glanced to the right and noticed Homad's domes. Browna stepped out of one. She glowered. "Where have you been? I haven't seen you lately."

I answered. To my left, M4 and Hae Lana appeared.

"How did we end up here?" blurted Hae Lana.

"My MAW is trying to answer that but it will take time."

Browna scowled. "Adam, M-Four, and Hae Lana, you missed the earthquake."

I blinked, dumbfounded. "When did it happen?"

Browna began staring at me, amazed. "This morning, about five hours ago."

Hae Lana shook her head. "All these events are freakish, hard to analyze."

Browna glowered. "What events?"

Hae Lana mentioned the Yaan.

Browna narrowed her eyes. "Your explanation is outlandish."

Hae Lana sighed. "I hardly believe it myself. It defies explanation."

Far away, a rumbling became louder.

"According to my MAW, pressure inside the volcano is building up."

Hae Lana glared at her. "Are you sure? We're miles away from it."

"Seventy-one percent sure."

Hae Lana scowled. "That means there is a twenty-nine percent chance that you are wrong."

"Affirmative."

Hae Lana frowned. "And since a lot of trees and hills are in the way, seventy-one might be incorrect because it's based on too many assumptions."

Far away, smoke rose above the jungle. I pointed at it. "AF repaired my lenses a second ago. According to their MCIT, there is a forty-two percent chance that gas along with cinders are coming out of the volcano."

Hae Lana's eyes shifted back and forth. "Perhaps. AF repaired mine as well during that time. According to my lenses' MCIT, that assumption is forty-two percent correct."

Within minutes, volcanic ash drifted onto my shoulder. I flinched. "The dome has broken down. Why?"

"According to my MAW, mutated streptococcus along with viruses have destroyed twenty-three percent of it," said M4.

"That's impossible. Fane was well designed," snapped Hae Lana.

"The evidence speaks for itself."

I coughed. "The air is dirty. It's hard to breathe." A face mask along with a helmet came out of my shoulder pads. I inhaled filtered air. "That's better."

Wo Ra sprinted out of dome C. "There are holes in the ceiling. Ash is falling. The air is filled with it." She cleared her throat. "It is hard to breathe."

"I can repair that," M4 volunteered. She yanked a disk that was one-eighth-of-an-inch in diameter out of her belt, then handed it to Wo Ra.

"What is this for?"

"Place it on your chest."

She did. The disk, a compressed suit, along with a helmet and face mask, expanded, then covered her from head to toe. "Now I can breathe."

Soaa and Xa Om stepped out of another dome. Both of them mentioned the dirty air.

M4 handed both of them disks, too. Each disk expanded, covering them from head to toe.

Everything melted, then vanished. To my left, M4 was standing in a field. Ahead of me, about one hundred fifty yards away, sixteen Civil War soldiers, men in blue, all with ancient rifles, darted toward us.

"M-Four, where is the rest of the crew?"

"At this point, unknown." She changed into a Civil War soldier, a man who resembled the sixteen. She remarked, "Adam. If you don't change your suit, these entities will become suspicious."

"Good point." It turned into an outfit that was similar to theirs.

CHAPTER THIRTY-FIVE

They arrived. The tallest, a sergeant, glared at me. "Private, Grant's men are coming. When they arrive, fire at will."

I paused, amazed that my mind had translated his speech. Then I clenched my teeth, scared by this event. To my right all sixteen hunkered down behind a small hill, rifles aimed. I stared at them, caught off guard. "M-Four, according to my lenses, Grant was a Union general."

"Affirmative."

The sergeant pointed at us. He shouted, "Get down. Otherwise you'll be an easy target for Grant's men."

Both of us rushed behind the hill, dove to the ground, then peeked over the hill.

Two hundred yards away, a large group of men, all in gray uniforms, ran out of a forest and sprinted this way.

The sergeant shouted his orders, "We're outnumbered. When you see the whites of their eyes, fire."

I winced.

The sergeant pointed at us. "Where are your Henry rifles?"

"We lost them," M4 replied.

"You'll be dead soon," barked the sergeant at us. He turned to the solider beside him. "Corporal Lest. Are there any spare rifles?"

He glowered. "No sir."

Ahead, the men in gray shouted.

My adrenaline pumped harder. To our right, the men in blue discharged their weapons with a deafening sound. Ahead, the men in gray did the same.

Beams from M4 and my weapons, INSGS, struck two men in gray's chests. Both screamed and collapsed. Everything broke into fragments.

To my right, Xa Om appeared, saying "Adam, M-Four, both of you disappeared about fifteen minutes ago. Where did you go?"

I answered.

Xa Om flinched.

"Wow," Wo Ra said.

Croll stepped out of dome E. He frowned. "Both of you are back. A few minutes ago Hae Lana told me both of you vanished. The idea was too fantastic for me to accept. What happened?"

I mentioned the battle.

Croll rubbed his chin. "Unusual. Can you explain what is going on?"

"My MAW is organizing video recordings, photos, three-dimensional holographic probes, and neutrino scans. It may come up with an answer soon."

Croll blinked. "Adam, judging by that look on your face you're as amazed by your recent experience on that battlefield as I am."

"It's true. My lenses are sorting through possible explanations but the only answer they've come up with so far is that an informed response is pending."

Croll shook his head. "A pending informed response isn't any help right now." He sighed. "Unfortunately, your lenses' response is identical to mine. There must be a logical explanation for your disappearance."

Hae Lana stepped out of dome G. She frowned. "Adam, M-Four, Xa Om told me about your absence before I took a nap. Why did you vanish? You must have an answer."

M4 repeated my explanation.

Hae Lana shook her head. "Your answer is an excuse. You

can do better than that."

I bit my lip, irritated by her statement. "We're working on it."

Hae Lana's forehead tightened. "You better hurry. We need answers, not shitty excuses."

"Lava is coming this way," M4 said. "Quantum probability charts indicate that it should arrive in twenty-one minutes."

Chills ran across my spine. "Fane won't change its shape or take off. We must hike toward higher ground."

"Won't change its shape or take off? Are you sure?" exclaimed Hae Lana.

"Yes."

She glowered. "Have you tried several times?"

I bit my lip, irritated by her remark. "Yes."

Hae Lana gnashed her teeth. "What caused this?"

"According to three diagnostic tests, alien viruses have destroyed nine of the ship's bio-circuits," said M4.

"I thought that Fane was designed to overcome these problems."

"It was designed to overcome six billion three million of them."

Hae Lana frowned. "But not this one."

"Let's go," I said. "My lenses just contacted those who are inside their domes." Everybody else stepped out of them and the entire group hiked.

Soon we passed kapoks.

To my left, Croll sighed. "I had to leave two of my MCITS behind."

Hae Lana glowered. "Shit. Will that make it harder to determine Isal's orbit around its star?"

Croll's brow tightened. "It will."

"If our group doesn't reach our destination in fifteen minutes everybody will die because changes based on initial conditions indicate that the lava will arrive in fifteen minutes and three seconds," said M4.

"Don't slow down."

Hae Lana glared at Croll. "I'm aware of that. Your comment is useless."

"Stop giving me a hard time."

I stood between them. "Stop arguing."

"I'm trying to help," protested Croll.

"Trying to help? What a bunch of shit," snapped Hae Lana.

I gave them both a stern look. "Stop arguing. Focus on reaching higher ground."

"I smell smoke," said Wo Ra.

"Three quantum probability charts point out that lava is burning adjacent parts of the Glorm," commented M4.

Xa Om coughed. "The smoke is getting thicker."

"I just sent new computer code into everybody's face masks. In a few seconds, they will improve. As a result the entire crew can breathe without coughing," M4 told us.

Hae Lana coughed. "Hurry up." She tripped, then gagged.

I winced. "You look terrible, might choke to death."

Hae Lana wheezed.

I reached out, grabbed her hand, then pulled her up.

M4 scanned her. "Two probability graphs indicate that she will recover soon."

"It doesn't look that way to me," exclaimed Croll.

I said, "Hae Lana, I hate watching you die."

Soaa cringed.

Wo Ra flinched.

Hae Lana inhaled. "I feel better now."

"Good," said Xa Om.

"Hae Lana, you frightened me," Wo Ra said.

Croll nodded. "That was too close for comfort,"

Hae Lana blurted, "No shit."

"The lava will arrive in eight minutes and nineteen

seconds," M4 informed us.

Ahead, in the near distance, thick smoke went around strangler figs. Everything swirled, then vanished.

CHAPTER THIRTY-SIX

To my right, M4 stepped over grass. "We're in a field."
A rumbling grew louder. I winced. "What's making that noise?"

"My MAW is probing, trying to come up with an answer."

About two hundred yards away, six vehicles drove over a hill, headed our way.

I winced. "According to my lenses, those are tiger tanks."

M4 nodded. "My MAW probe indicates that your lenses are correct."

My body went cold. "How did we end up here?"

"Unfortunately, I don't have an answer. Two graphs, both based on Bayesian probabilities, are inconclusive."

"Where is Hae Lana and everybody else?"

"At this point, unknown."

German soldiers rushed out from behind the tigers. "Achtung," one yelled.

I winced. "Lets alter our appearance. Otherwise they'll shoot us."

"Altering them is a beneficial idea." M4 changed into a male.

Our suits turned into gray uniforms. Our helmets vanished and were replaced by German ones.

I blenched. "Let's hope this works."

The German soldiers rushed past us. One shouted at us. "Beeilung."

My lenses translated — "Hurry up."

A tank rumbled by. M4 and I spun around. A screeching became louder.

"Hit the dirt," M4 said. "An artillery shell is coming."

Both of us dove to the ground. On our left, about eighty yards away, a tank exploded.

I cringed. "A shell hit it."

M4 agreed. "Three computer models indicate that you are correct."

As smoke poured out of the machine, German soldiers rushed around it. Soon a screeching grew louder.

My adrenaline pumped harder. "Another shell is coming."

"It will hit a location that is on our right, sixteen feet, eight inches from us," calculated M4.

Everything faded and was replaced by the Glorm.

To my right Hae Lana scowled. "Adam, a couple of minutes ago you and M-Four vanished. Why?"

"I wish I knew. M-Four, can you answer her question?"

"Unfortunately, I cannot."

"I want answers."

"Hae Lana, you must wait for a thorough analysis."

She glared at the robot. "That's a shitty excuse."

"It's a fact, not an excuse."

"Let's hike to the right and climb that hill," I said.

Hae Lana examined the hill. "It's steep. Going in that direction will slow us down."

"That's an order."

Hae Lana glared at me. "Yes sir."

Everybody veered in that direction and began scaling it. To my right, Wo Ra tripped and rolled downhill. Behind us, a rumbling grew louder. I glanced in that direction as lava moved toward the bottom of the slope.

CHAPTER THIRTY-SEVEN

"Assist me," yelled Wo Ra.

I turned, rushed toward her, then stooped, grabbed my new friend's wrist, stood and hiked uphill. In front of me, Hae Lana bellowed, "Adam, Wo Ra, hurry, you're ten feet ahead of the lava."

I blenched and slogged on while my back became hotter.

"The heat. I feel like I am on fire," blurted Wo Ra.

Our group reached the top of the hill. To our left and right, lava flowed around the bottom. A kapok fell over. Hae Lana hopped on it and walked. Others stepped on it. Then one by one, they followed her, bound for the side of another hill.

Everything faded. To my left, M4 and Xa Om took a few steps. I flinched. "Where is everybody else?"

"At this point, unknown," M4 said.

I blinked. "What does your MAW indicate?"

"Its screens are filled with random, useless algorithms."

"What are alga-algorithms?" Xa Om asked.

"They are—"

"Let's talk about that another time," I blurted.

Xa Om paused, his forehead tight.

Leaves on nearby trees, all of them in a dense jungle, shook, blown by the wind. I blinked, surprised by this sudden change. "Where are we?"

"According to nearby strangler figs, we're on Yerak," said Xa Om.

"According to my MCIT created star map, that is correct," confirmed M4.

I winced. "Xa Om, do they know who or what sent us here?"

"No."

"What else are the figs saying?"

"I'm not sure yet. What is the best way to say it? Intra-intro-interpreting their comments will take awhile."

I bit my lip, annoyed.

"I know this area. My village was here."

"What happened to it?" asked M4.

"According to the adjacent lupunas, nine years ago, the Kicra slaughtered every Ditu. Then the Kicra destroyed all the huts."

I blenched. "That's horrible."

Xa Om started trembling. "Thinking about it shocks me."

"According to my MAW, five Kicra are on our left, sixty yards and two feet away, advancing in this direction."

I flinched. "Let's get out of here." Our small party hiked to the right and went between towering Pallas.

On my left, Xa Om said, "There is something different about this part of the Weon."

I blinked, taken aback. "What is it?"

"There used to be hundreds of wimba. But they're gone. Now this location is full of fucus."

"The Weon has changed," said M4.

"That is true. However, those trees usually lasted for hundreds of years. I know that because when I was younger, they told me so," remarked Xa Om.

"You knew them well."

"Yes. It took years of practice, but I learned how to talk and listen to them."

I paused, curious. "What are these fucus saying?"

"That we, a group of newcomers, are emitting a strong odor, one that the Kicra can follow."

My body went cold.

Xa Om sighed. "Being here reminds me of Ze Ma."

"It's horrible that she is gone," I said.

Xa Om frowned. "I'm trying not to think about it too much."

"Why are you trying to do that?" M4 asked.

"If I did, it would be hard to walk, listen, talk or do anything because the grief would be too much to handle."

I nodded. "I know what you mean."

"According to my MAW, those Kicra are on our left, will reach this location in six minutes and eleven seconds," commented M4.

I blenched. "According to my lenses, this open space is the only safe area within a radius of one hundred yards. When they arrive fire at will."

"There are eleven more Kicra on our right."

My adrenaline began pumping. "How far away are they?"

"Two-hundred-three yards and nine inches."

Xa Om flinched. "This is ghastly."

I imagined these predators tearing us apart.

Behind us, a soft, barely audible crunching grew louder.

Everybody spun around.

CHAPTER THIRTY-EIGHT

In the near distance, three Kicra halted, saliva dripping off their jaws. Beams from our weapons struck them. They screeched. *Eeeeok.* Suddenly, all three turned left, rushed into the jungle and vanished, hidden in shadows.

"M-Four, are they coming back?" I asked.

"At this point, unknown."

"According to nearby fucus, the Kicra will stop eighty yards from here, on our right. When more arrive all of them will attack our group," said Xa Om.

My stomach muscles tightened. "Why are they so eager to kill us?"

"I asked several wimba. They told me that the Kicra think of us as invaders. As a result, we must die."

I winced. Everything faded. To my left, M4 raised her arm.

On my right, Hae Lana glowered. "Where is the rest of the crew?"

"At this point, unknown," M4 answered.

In front of our crew, my father stepped out of our house.

I blinked, astounded. "Dad. How are you?"

He glared at me. "Who are you?"

My body went cold. "Adam, your son."

"I don't have a son. Your joke is cruel. Go away before I call the police." He turned, stepped inside and the door closed.

I hesitated, my body trembling.

"An unexpected event," commented M4.

"That was fucking weird," blurted Hae Lana. "Your own father didn't recognize you. Something is wrong."

I paused, caught off guard.

"What do you mean something is wrong?"

Hae Lana glowered at the robot. "This house resembles many on Laasp. But something about the street, the roof and windows is different."

"Hae Lana, your statements are correct. My MAW is organizing data, trying to determine why they are different."

Hae Lana frowned. "Damn right, I'm correct. My lenses are sorting archives, trying to get to the bottom of this odd situation."

I pointed at the sky. "There are two sun-like stars, not one." Laasp only had one.

M4 nodded. "Affirmative."

Hae Lana nodded. "Yet it's so similar. How could that be? That doesn't make sense. There must be a prudent explanation."

"If you come up with a prudent one, tell me what it is," said M4.

Hae Lana glared at her. "Don't be a wiseass."

"Since there are two stars, I conclude that this isn't Laasp."

Hae Lana frowned. "For the sake of argument, let's say that your statement is a fact. If it is, are we in a computer program?"

"At this point, unknown. My MAW's recent probes are inconclusive."

Hae Lana scowled. "Or did a machine or somebody transport our party to another planet?"

I paused, weighing options.

M4 paused, too. "Fascinating question. However, my MAW is still organizing probabilities. As a result, providing an informed answer at this point is impossible."

Hae Lana frowned. "When you come up with an informed one, let me know. My lenses are struggling with that question. Damn, I hate the uncertainty. Adam, judging by that look on your face, you're as baffled as I am."

"That is true."

"According to my MAW's statistics, an asteroid will strike this planet in nine years, two days and nine seconds. The asteroid will destroy all life on it."

I winced. Everything became grey and broke apart. To my right and left, lava flowed around the bottom of the hill.

To my left, Croll remarked, "Adam, you, M-Four, Xa Om, and Hae Lana disappeared a few minutes ago. Why?"

Xa Om told him.

Croll frowned.

My mind raced, surprised by his comment. I talked about our recent experience.

Croll blinked. "My god."

To my right, Wo Ra raised her shaky hand. "The heat."

I pointed straight ahead. "There is a small gap between the lava flow. If we rush through it, everybody can reach another hill."

"I can't see the gap," blurted Hae Lana.

"Kapoks are blocking your view," I replied. Hae Lana took a few steps. "Now I see it."

Everybody but me darted toward it.

Hae Lana glanced over her shoulder. "Adam, what are you waiting for?"

"I want to make sure that everybody else makes it across."

Hae Lana blinked. "If you say so. The gap is disappearing. Shit. You'll have to jump over the lava."

I sprinted, hopped, and landed on the next hill.

To my left, Hae Lana winced. "I didn't think you would make it."

I raised my shaky hand. "Either did I."

Both of us sprinted uphill, following the others. To our right, lava flowed between fucus.

On my left, Hae Lana pointed at the lava. "Watch out."

My mind sped up. "I see it." Ahead smoke engulfed bushes.

To my left, M4 pointed to the right. "Two Teogs are coming this way. According to three probability graphs, they will arrive in five minutes and three seconds."

Next to M4, Soaa cringed.

Shivers went up my spine. "Are they going to attack our group or are they trying to escape the lava and don't care about us?"

M4 shook her head. "My probability charts need more time to answer that."

In front of her Hae Lana shouted, "Shit, Teogs again. I hate them."

Next to her, Croll barked, "I'll kill them with a couple of shots."

Browna yelled, "Seeing them in this smoke will be tough."

Hae Lana prepared to shoot a couple of them. "I have quick reflexes."

"Let's hope so," remarked Browna.

"You'll see."

Behind Hae Lana, Soaa coughed.

On Hae Lana's left, M4 said, "Hae Lana, you should weigh options carefully before acting."

"Do you think I'm a fool?"

"Of course not."

"Then stop making dumb comments. I am careful, know what I am doing."

"As you wish."

Ahead, burning trees blocked our path.

To my right, Croll hollered, "Shocking."

Everybody rushed around them.

On my left, Xa Om winced. Next to him Wo Ra flinched.

Not far beyond them, Hae Lana called out, "The heat is wearing me out."

"Don't slow down," I yelled. Wo Ra tripped and fell. My adrenaline pumped harder. I grabbed her arm, lifted her then ran. To my right, smoke poured out of bushes. In the opposite direction, a distant squawking became louder.

Ahead, Hae Lana shouted, "What made that noise?"

"A Teog?" replied M4 behind me.

To my left, Soaa cleared her throat.

"Is it going to kill us or is it hurt?" Hae Lana asked.

"Unknown."

"Damn it, I want answers."

Our crew hopped over smoldering weeds. To our right, faraway, a booming grew louder.

"Is that the volcano?" Hae Lana called out.

"According to my MAW, it is."

"Damn."

"T-trouble," announced Soaa.

In front of us, lava poured to the left, moving through a six-foot-wide gully. Croll halted. "Jumping across this looks dangerous."

Next to him, Hae Lana called out, "Do it. There's no other route available."

Croll took a few steps back, rushed forward, leaped, and ended up on the side of a hill. Without warning, he stumbled, fell, then rolled downhill. When he stopped, Croll stood, and darted uphill.

"Shit, Croll that was close," Hae Lana hollered.

He nodded. "Jump, before the lava flow becomes wider."

CHAPTER THIRTY-NINE

Hae Lana ran, leaped, and ended up in dirt, a foot from the lava. "Shit." Croll grabbed her hand, and both of them darted up hill.

I was the last to cross. I bit my lip, scared.

On the opposite side, Soaa yelled, "Hu-hurry, the lava flow is getting wider every second."

I exhaled, trying to relax, then dashed forward, sprang and landed next to M4. She grabbed my arm and jerked me forward.

On my left, Croll remarked, "Your right heel missed the lava by an inch."

I pictured my body in the lava and getting burned. Our group trekked.

To my right, Hae Lana glowered. "Adam, judging by that look on your face, something scared you."

I exhaled, relieving tension. "The lava did." On our left, somewhere in the smoke, a crunching grew louder.

Hae Lana flinched. "What is making that noise?"

I glanced in that direction. In the near distance, a ten-foot-high, sixty-foot-long, four-legged silhouette walked between lupunas. The creature was barely visible in the haze.

"It's coming this way," Hae Lana called out.

"It moves slowly. According to statistics it is harmless," said M4.

Hae Lana raised her arm, ready to fire her weapon. "Harmless? I don't think so."

"Wait, don't shoot," I yelled.

Hae Lana flinched. "It's close. There are spikes on its back. Don't shoot? Are you sure?"

"Yes, hold your fire."

Hae Lana sniffed, "It smells like weeds."

The creature groaned.

"Its entire body is covered by leathery skin. Graphs indicate that there is eighty-two percent chance that this unfamiliar species is a reptile," said M4.

Hae Lana aimed her arm, ready to discharge her INSG. "I've never seen a reptile that was as big and odd as this one."

"An intriguing genus."

"Its mouth is full of weeds."

Soon the creature veered to the right, moving slowly, went between lupunas, kept going and vanished, hidden by bushes.

Hae Lana scowled. "Intriguing? M-Four, is that the best you can come up with?"

"Affirmative."

"M-Four, you're useless. I want answers."

"Sorry."

Hae Lana scowled. "Sorry isn't good enough."

M4 paused, stone-faced while her MAW clicked softly, gathering information.

Hae Lana frowned. "Did you hear me?"

"Of course."

"Then say something."

"I'm busy."

"Leave M-Four alone," I told Hae Lane. "She is collecting data."

Hae Lana glared at me. "She needs to do a better job."

"That's an order. Leave her alone."

Hae Lana gnashed her teeth and continued walking.

Ahead, Soaa brushed embers off her shoulder.

Hae Lana scowled. "Adam, why can't M-Four come up with answers faster?"

My stomach muscles tightened. "Because she needs more information."

Hae Lana glared at me. "It's time to shut her down and leave her behind."

I bit my lip, angry. "That is a bad idea."

"You're too sentimental."

I shook my head. "Like I said, it's a bad idea."

Croll glowered. "Hae Lana has a point."

I glared at them. "Both of you, knock it off. Otherwise, M-Four can't do her job."

Croll pointed at me. "Adam you're tired. I'm qualified to take over."

"I'm more qualified than Croll is," barked Hae Lana.

I clenched my teeth, upset by their attitudes. "Croll, you used to be more reasonable. Why did you change?"

He glared at me, then mumbled incoherently.

On my right, Browna interrupted them. "Croll, Hae Lana, both of you are too temperamental and unfit to lead."

I nodded. Suddenly, flames engulfed the surrounding trees. "Stoop, then walk straight ahead. That is the only safe route available."

"Shit, shit, shit," exclaimed Hae Lana.

CHAPTER FORTY

Everybody followed my order. In front of me, Croll pointed to the right. "That is a safe route. Let's go that way."

I put my hand up. "No, go straight ahead."

"That is a bad plan." Croll darted to the right.

"Come back here."

"Everybody should follow me."

My adrenaline pumped faster. "Do as you're told."

"You aren't listening to me." Flame covered branches dropped on his head and shoulders. He screamed. "Somebody . . ." The fire spread, then engulfed him.

To my left, Browna hollered, "Oh my god."

Xa Om rushed toward Croll and stopped. "It's too hot."

"Xa Om, come back here or you'll die," I said.

Croll, a walking torch, took a few steps then collapsed.

Xa Om returned, spun around, and walked straight ahead. "If only I could have saved him."

"It's too late. Everybody, keep going. Hike straight ahead," I said.

Next to Xa Om, Hae Lana blurted, "Croll is gone."

Behind them, Soaa remarked, "Ye-yes." She grabbed Xa Om's trembling hand. "Xa Om, don't stop or you'll end up like Dr. Croll."

"Okay."

Within minutes, our group reached open space, then stood. Browna rubbed her back. "Hiking in a stooped position hurts my back. I'm glad that is over."

Hae Lana tried to soothe her back, too. "My back still hurts."

"Adam, everybody, there is a Teog on our left," remarked Soaa.

Chills went up my spine. "I don't see it."

"Ne-nearby lupunas can. According to them, it's about eighty yards away."

Xa Om sighed. "More stress."

Next to him, Wo Ra's hands kept trembling.

M4 noticed. "Wo Ra, you're shaking."

"I am scared."

"If only we could bury Dr. Croll," remarked Browna.

I cringed, shocked by my colleague's death. "Burying his corpse is a good idea. However, there isn't enough time."

Hae Lana glowered. "Adam, you left Dr. Croll behind."

I bit my lip. "If we go back, everybody will die."

Hae Lana glared at me. Then she looked straight ahead. Our group kept going and went around burning weeds. "Can't we move any faster?"

"It's too dangerous."

Everybody stooped, then trekked. Above us, flames raced across branches.

"M-misery," commented Soaa.

Next to her, Xa Om said, "This is the only safe route left."

Behind her, M4 nodded. "Affirmative."

Within minutes, everybody came upon another open space and all of us stood.

M4 glanced to the right and left. "The lava has stopped moving."

Wo Ra examined her shaky hand.

Browna looked at Wo Ra's hands, too. "Stopped. That's great."

Behind us, far away, a hooting became louder.

"What's making that sound? It sounds like an owl," blurted Hae Lana.

"A Bolra is warning another creature, telling it to go away," said Wo Ra.

"Wo Ra, you're just a kid. How would you know that?"

"Wo Ra is perceptive," explained Xa Om.

Hae Lana shook her head. "She is a child. A bird made that noise."

"According to my MAW, Wo Ra is correct," said M4.

Hae Lana scowled. "M-Four, you're malfunctioning, don't know what you're talking about."

I sighed. "Hae Lana, stop arguing."

She stared at me, her jaw muscles tensed. "I'm pointing out the obvious. If you are as alert as I am, you would be aware of this."

Browna glowered. "Hae Lana, you argue too much."

"I'm not, I'm pointing out the obvious. All of you are tired, aren't paying attention."

I snapped, "Hae Lana, that's enough."

She paused, her jaw muscles clenched.

On our left, far beyond palmettos, somewhere in the haze, a barely audible scratching grew louder.

Hae Lana turned toward the noise. "What made that sound?"

"Wha-what made it? According to a nearby pallas, a Teog is stalking us," said Soaa.

Xa Om nodded. "That is true."

Hae Lana shook her head. "According to my lenses, it's the wind. Everybody is on edge, overreacting."

"Keep hiking," I said.

Within minutes, the smell of rotten garbage became stronger.

"Add adjacent grass has pointed out that a Teog is still

close by," said Soaa.

Hae Lana glared at her. "You're telling me that grass is pointing this out? That's ridiculous."

"Ye-yes, it is telling me that."

Hae Lana scowled. "Does anybody else believe you?"

"I do," replied Xa Om

Wo Ra stood beside her father. "So do I."

Browna nodded. "Xa Om and Wo Ra are alert. I believe them."

I nodded, too. "Yes, they are alert."

Hae Lana sighed. "All of you are fooling yourselves."

"Hae Lana, we aren't. You should be—how shall I put it— more reasonable," remarked Xa Om.

"I am being more reasonable. However, the rest of you aren't."

"According to a lupuna, the Teog has left," said Wo Ra.

Hae Lana's brow tightened. "That is wrong. The Teog wasn't there in the first place."

My stomach muscles tightened. Behind me, a distant whooping grew louder. I flinched. "What is making that sound?"

M4 shook her head. "Unknown."

"According to a wimba, a Groowla is," commented Wo Ra.

"What is a Groowla?" asked Browna.

Wo Ra tilted her head. "The wimba did not say anything else about it."

Hae Lana tittered. "Ridiculous. It's another fairy tale animal."

At dusk, after hiking for hours, our group set up camp, one I named Sefan. Xa Om passed around leaves, our meal.

Browna took a bite, chewed, and swallowed. "They taste like paper."

Hae Lana munched. "Yes, like paper. I wish we had

something better."

"Xa Om, thank you. The spirit of Glorm has been kind enough to offer food," remarked Wo Ra.

Xa Om smiled. "You are welcome, my child. However, you sound sad."

"I am. I miss my mother."

Xa Om sighed. "So do I."

"She was always helpful and loving."

Xa Om began to sing, "Lo ey, Lo aw. Me trieste."

"What do those words mean?" Browna asked.

M4 translated. "It's a song dedicated to dead Ditu fathers, deceased mothers and children who have passed away. It's designed to comfort the living."

"It's a mournful tune," I noted.

Browna frowned. "It is."

Hae Lana bit her lip. "It reminds me of Eaaga and Croll." She rose and walked away.

Hae Lana, where are you going?" I asked.

"I need some time alone."

"Don't go too far," I called out. "We want to keep track of you."

"I'm a grown up. Don't worry about me."

Browna sighed. "She won't listen."

I took a deep breath, trying to relax. "I know. She is a great scientist but can be stubborn."

"Tell me about it. I'm surprised that she is still alive. One of these days she will mess up and end up dead or hurt," Browna said.

I bit my lip.

"Adam, you look irritated," Browna remarked.

"I am. Hae Lana gets on my nerves."

Browna's jaw muscles bulged. "I know what you mean."

"Some wimba have pointed out that a Groowla is coming this way," said Xa Om.

Browna flinched. "Is it a predator?"

"I-I can't tell. Is that the best word, words? Yes."

CHAPTER FORTY-ONE

After eating several leaves, I looked around. "Hae Lana, where are you?"

"She is ignoring you," said Browna.

"Maybe." I called out her name again.

Browna scowled. "She'll return soon. She needs to be alone for a few minutes."

I blinked. "Xa Om, M-Four, help me search for her."

Browna's forehead tightened. "Is that necessary?"

"It's better to be safe than sorry."

Browna shrugged. "If you say so."

Our small group departed. Xa Om pointed north. "According to nearby palmettos, she went in this direction."

I nodded.

"My MAW can't locate her," said M4.

My stomach muscles tightened. "Why not?"

"It could be a variety of factors. The surrounding air is filled with viruses and mutated staphylococcus. Both have destroyed nine percent of the MAW's bio-circuits."

I bit my lip. "Can the MAW repair itself?"

"It's doing that. However, that procedure takes time."

I blinked, frustrated. "How much time?"

"Minutes or hours. It's hard to say."

I winced. "How many viruses are there?"

"Six-thousand-nineteen per cubic foot."

My mind raced, trying to figure out what to do about these potentially lethal organisms.

"Judging by that expression on your face, something is

bothering you," commented M4.

"Hae Lana usually responds to my calls."

"Your colleague is an independent soul, doesn't like following orders," said Xa Om.

I nodded. "That's true. However, since she is the responsible type, something about her long absence feels wrong."

Xa Om pointed ahead. "According to strangler figs, she is half a mile ahead."

I winced. "That's odd. It would have been easier for her to hike a short distance, sit and relax, not travel that far."

"I agree," said M4.

"She might have been restless, wanted to explore," commented Xa Om.

"Maybe. However, this area is thick and dark, hard to travel through," I said.

Far away, to our left, a rustling grew louder. I flinched. "What made that noise?"

M4 scanned the area. "Unknown."

"According to a fucus, a flock of winged roaches touched down on vines," said Xa Om.

I cringed. "Winged roaches. How many are there?"

"Unknown. The fucus didn't say."

"What stinks? Something smells like stomach bile."

"My MAW's screen is blank, can't provide any information," M4 replied.

"I can't interpret what adjacent shiringas are saying."

Behind us, a barely-audible faint shuffling grew louder. I glanced over my shoulder, wanting to locate where it was coming from, but only noticed dimly lit fucus and bushes. "What is making that sound?"

To my right, Xa Om said, "According to nearby strangler figs, a Teog is following us."

My body went cold. "I can't see it. How far away is it?"

"Ninety yards."

I raised my arm, ready to fire.

"It's moving to our left."

"A sneaky tactic," remarked M4.

I looked ahead. "Let's keep going. I want to find Hae Lana."

"A superb idea."

Soon we hiked through an ankle deep stream, one filled with five-foot-long eels. Two opened their jaws. Beams from our weapons struck their mouths. They shrieked. *Veeeot.*

I cringed. "These creatures smell like garbage."

"Affirmative," commented M4.

Xa Om said, "I'm glad we killed them. They're vicious."

As chills ran up my spine, our group reached the opposite shore and slogged on.

On my left, Xa Om shoved two-inch-long flies off his wrist. "I het-hate this part of the Glorm. It's gloomy and these parasites keep biting me."

I pushed several off my fingers. "They're sucking my blood."

"They're sucking mine as well," remarked Xa Om.

"Xa Om, although your accent is thick, your English is improving."

"Yours is thick as well."

I shrugged.

"Your language is full of tech, how shall I say it, technicul . . . technicol . . . technical terms, isn't always easy to understand."

"In my humble opinion, it isn't technical enough," said M4.

"A lupuna just told me that your friend is sixteen mooloos away. In other words, sixteen feet away," said Xa Om.

I winced. "It's too dim. I don't see her."

Xa Om pointed ahead. "Go straight."

My mind sped up, weighing options. To my right, M4

grabbed huge leaves, and tossed them aside, revealing Hae Lana.

I winced. "She is covered by dried mucus. Hae Lana, can you move?"

She blinked.

"Our colleague can't," remarked M4.

CHAPTER FORTY-TWO

Our beams struck the mucus, tearing some of it apart. M4 stooped. Her right hand changed into a saw, then started cutting.

I winced. "Be careful. Don't slice her skin off."

"My cutting tool is accurate to one millionth of an inch."

Behind us, a faint rustling grew louder.

I spun around with my arm raised, ready to fire. "What is making that noise?"

On my left, Xa Om said, "According to a wimba, a Teog is twenty feet away from us, waiting for the right moment to strike."

My adrenaline pumped harder. "It's dark, impossible to see the creature."

"The beast is use-using that to keep you confused."

I imagined the creature racing toward me and biting my arm off.

Behind me, M4 said, "I'm almost finished."

I looked at Xa Om. "Keep your arm steady, ready to shoot."

"I will. However, my aim is ah . . . lousy."

I flinched. "Your INSG should hit the beast on the first shot."

A laser beam came out of Xa Om's weapon and hit dirt. "It missed the target. I don't know why."

My stomach muscles tightened. I looked over my shoulder. Nanites came out of M-Four's waist, then formed a small platform. She grabbed our colleague's body, then put it on the platform. "For whatever reason, Hae Lana can't or won't talk."

My body went cold. "She looks horrible. Let's head for Sefan."

Our group departed, hiking slowly. To our right, the Teog rushed out of the shadows.

"It's a coming," shouted Xa Om.

Our beams hit the creature. It howled. *Yaaaaow.*

While my mind sped up, trying to anticipate the creature's next move, the predator spun around, and darted behind a wall of vines. "Where is it?"

"A palmetto just told me that it's hiding behind kapoks, is a-ah-about forty feet away," replied Xa Om.

My mind sped up, weighing options. "Is it following us?"

"No. It's standing."

I blinked. "Did we injure it?"

"Hard to say. I'm trying to decipher the palmettos other comments."

I bit my lip, frustrated. "M-Four, why isn't Hae Lana talking?"

"At this point, unknown. When we reach camp, my MAW will scan her more thoroughly. However, it isn't designed to diagnose humans or any other race's brainwaves."

I clenched my teeth, scared. "Browna will know more."

"There is some swelling on Hae Lana's forehead," said M4.

Shivers went up my spine. "It looks like a bump. Is she suffering from head trauma?"

"Unknown."

My lenses dialed Browna's number. She didn't answer. I winced. "Browna's lenses won't accept my call."

"They won't accept mine either," M4 said.

"Mine have detected—how you say—static," remarked Xa Om.

I paused, disappointed. "M-Four, how many times have yours tried to reach her or any crew since we left Sefan?"

"Six."

"I've tried to call her five times since we left. The only thing I heard was sta-static," said Xa Om.

I bit my lip in frustrated.

Our group came upon kapoks we had passed before. To my right, behind nearby dangling creepers, a faint rustling grew louder. I winced. "Is the Teog making that sound?"

Ahead, Xa Om replied, "Palmettos sa-say it is."

"Xa Om, you're stuttering, sounds like you're frightened."

"It's true."

Next to him, M4 said, "Shooting at a creature we can't see is futile."

I winced. "Yes."

Xa Om flinched. "If there was only something we could do to scare it away."

M4 nodded. "Affirmative. However, achieving that goal is difficult."

I aimed to the right, then fired at a palmetto.

Xa Om jerked. "Why did-did you do that?"

"To scare the Teog away."

Xa Om coughed. "A lupuna said the beast is following us, hiding behind pallas."

My mind sped up, trying to come up with another option.

We reached camp, then entered dome F. M4 placed Hae Lana face up on a bed. Soaa rushed inside. She frowned. "Sha-she keeps staring into space. What's wrong?"

"Based on my latest MAW scan, she is in a coma," M4 said.

Soaa blenched. "I-I have more bad news. Browna vanished a few minutes after you, Adam, M-Four and Hae Lana departed."

I cringed. "Did anybody look for her?"

Soaa clenched her teeth. "Sha-she told me she would be

close by, gathering edible leaves. I assumed it wouldn't take much time to do this. Not long after she left, I called out her name. She didn't answer. Then my lenses called her. Unfortunately, the only thing they detected was white noise."

My mind sped up, trying to come up with a solution.

Wo Ra entered, trembling. "I heard that. Minutes ago, sabal said that Teog's spray venom into their prey's mouth. As a result, their prey lapses into a deep sleep for several days. Before they wake up, the creature bites off their head, and eats it. It devours the rest of the body later."

Soaa's eyes widened. "Ga-ghastly."

Wo Ra flinched. "I cannot look at her anymore. It is too painful." She rushed out of the dome.

M4 examined Hae Lana again. "I don't have an antidote for this. If she wakes up, let's feed her."

My body went cold. "Feeding her is a good idea. I'll go outside and stand guard."

Hours later, M4 and I sat, facing the jungle.

"It's too bad that Hae Lana hasn't woken up," I said.

"Affirmative."

To our left, Soaa stepped out of a dome. She frowned. "I-I heard that. In ma-my doubtful moments, my guess is that she will never wake up."

"Two graphs indicate there is forty-five percent chance that she won't," said M4.

"Don't give up," I blurted.

Soaa ground her teeth together but didn't say anything.

"Soaa, M-Four, Wo Ra and I will look for Browna," I said. "You and Xa Om should watch over Hae Lana."

Soaa remarked, "Goh-good id-idea."

On our right, Xa Om and Wo Ra darted out of the jungle. Wo Ra stuck out her hand. "A palmetto told me that its leaves might help Hae Lana."

I took the leaves. "Great."

Xa Om grabbed my hand. "I'm worried that they might be poisonous."

"Wo Ra, do you place the leaves in her mouth or rub them against her skin?" asked M4.

"Place them in her mouth."

"If they work, how long will it take for her wake up?" Xa Om asked.

"I do not know," replied Wo Ra.

Xa Om scratched his chin. "Wo Ra do it. I have faith in you."

"Yes, father."

The young lady slowly inserted them in our colleague's mouth, then paused.

Xa Om glowered. "Nothing is happening."

I blinked, worried. "Let's wait."

Xa Om stuttered, "Very ga-good."

"M-Four, Wo Ra, let's search for Dr. Browna," I said.

Minutes later, all three of us hiked through the Glorm. "Wo Ra, did any of the adjacent wimba or other trees notice that Browna vanished?" I asked.

"No."

"It's odd that they didn't," M4 noted.

"I am not old enough to understand everything they are saying," said Wo Ra.

I stopped her. "You're mature for your age."

She grinned. "Thank you." Our group slogged on.

After passing bromeliads Wo Ra commented, "According to a palmetto, when Browna was two hundred yards from here, she vanished."

I blinked, caught off guard. "Vanished? Does that mean she ran away?"

Wo Ra paused. "It did not say."

"Did a Teog grab her?" M4 asked.

Wo Ra sighed. "It did not say."

My stomach muscles tightened. "Let's keep searching."

"This area is shadowy, creepy," said Wo Ra.

M4 commented, "Affirmative."

To our right, faraway, a whooshing grew louder.

I winced. "What made that noise?"

"Three wimba said it was a butterfly," replied Wo Ra.

"Interesting," said M4.

I looked ahead. "Let's hope the only species we encounter is a butterfly."

"Affirmative."

I turned to Wo Ra. "Did any of these strangler figs or other trees notice Browna's disappearance?"

"No. They are saying that our voices are loud, may attract Teogs or Bolras."

I flinched. "Let's whisper."

"Good idea," murmured M4.

Soon Wo Ra murmured, "Adam, your body has changed, it's sending out a cinnamon odor. This scent fools Bolras and Teogs. They assume it's coming from a bush."

I blinked, stunned by her comment.

Hours later, at dusk, we set up another camp, one with several domes. A chair popped out of one. I sat.

"It's too bad we can't find Dr. Browna," said M4.

I sighed. "That's true. Let's try again tomorrow."

M4 nodded.

My mind sped up, attempting to figure out what we could do to locate her. "I'll stand guard until two in the morning."

M4 agreed. "I'll examine photos, recordings, scans and holographic probes until then." She stepped inside a dome.

CHAPTER FORTY-THREE

Moments before midnight, as I yawned, an indigo silhouette, mostly hidden by leaves, crept toward me. It rushed in my direction. I aimed, then fired. The creature screeched. *Eeooot*. It knocked me to the left. I fell out of my chair, landed on my back, and sat up, blasting. It slashed my leg. A beam, coming from somebody else's weapon, struck it. *Eeooot*. It bit off the end of my pinky finger. As white-hot pain raced up my hand, another beam, coming from my left, struck its snout. *Eoooot*. The beast spun around and sprinted into the jungle.

On my left, M4 reached down, grabbed my arm, and pulled me up.

She aimed a wrist-mounted nozzle at my injured finger. "This is going to hurt."

I winced. "Go ahead."

She sprayed.

I flinched.

She looked at me. "The pain will go away in a minute. Unfortunately, mutated streptococcus has destroyed our best medications. This is all that is available."

As my hand throbbed, I nodded.

At dawn our group departed. Wo Ra winced. "What happened to your finger?"

I told her.

"Wow. I was asleep, never heard it," she blurted.

I shrugged. As distant insects chirped, we passed lines of

two-inch-long ants.

Wo Ra pointed at them, then cringed. "They are huge, scary."

"They're moving away from the volcano," M4 said.

At noon I said, "There is no sign of Browna anywhere."

M4 nodded. "Affirmative."

"Adam, Kapoks agree with you," commented Wo Ra.

I bit my lip, disappointed that our search party couldn't find her. "My lenses aren't receiving any calls from Xa Om or Soaa."

"I'm having the same problem," said M4.

Wo Ra reported the same issue.

"Let's head back to Sefan," I told them.

In the late afternoon, we reached it and stepped inside a dome. On a bed, Hae Lana cleared her throat.

I blinked. "Amazing. How do you feel?"

"Tired," she drawled.

"When did you wake up?"

She yawned. "About thirty minutes ago."

I gave her some coffee. After she took a sip, I asked, "Do you remember anything about the attack?"

"I wanted to take a short break and sat on a log in a shadowy area. Much to my surprise, mist struck my face. Then I felt dizzy and collapsed."

"Do you remember what happened after that?"

"No, damn it."

I paused, waiting for her to talk more.

On my right, Wo Ra sighed.

Hae Lana glowered. "How did you find me?"

I told her.

"It's hard for me to accept that the creature could sneak up on me."

"You were tired," I said.

"Even then, I should have been more alert."

"You made a mistake. That's all," M4 said.

"It was a stupid-ass mistake. What the fuck was I thinking?"

To my left, Wo Ra flinched.

"You shouldn't be so hard on yourself," M4 remarked.

"If I had been more alert, it wouldn't have knocked me out. Let's face it, I fucked up big time."

I paused, feeling that she wouldn't listen to more of our assurances.

"Like everybody else, I went through three-D holographic training for weeks. Then they put me along with others in a real jungle, a class, for two months. I passed with flying colors. It wasn't enough," Hae Lana said.

I mentioned that the three of us couldn't locate Browna.

"Why not?" she snapped.

Wo Ra explained the situation to Hae Lana.

"More fucking problems. One thing goes wrong. Then something else pops up."

"Do you feel strong enough to help us find her?" I asked.

She bit her lip. "I better." She rose to her feet and took a few steps, barely balanced.

M4 grabbed her arm. "Careful."

Hae Lana shook her head. "I'm a mess." She turned, walked slowly toward her bed, and collapsed face up on it. "I feel dizzy, need to rest."

M4 nodded. "Affirmative. You need to rest."

All three of us departed. In the near distance, Xa Om wiped sweat off his forehead. "It's hot."

"M-Four, Wo Ra, and I would like to keep searching for Dr. Browna. Can Soaa join us?" I asked Xa Om.

"I don't know where Soaa is."

My stomach muscles tensed up.

"I'll watch over Hae Lana while all three of you search for Dr. Browna."

I blenched, worried. When Wo Ra, M-Four, and I left camp, trying to find Dr. Browna, my lenses automatically recorded Dr. Browna in camp every six minutes along with everybody else. Unfortunately, after my lenses rang eight times, they stopped and were replaced by static. During that time, my lenses automatically sent emails to Dr. Browna and everybody in camp every fifteen minutes.

Their lenses didn't respond. As a result, my incoming receive email fields were blank. I was hoping that they sent me several three-D holograms. However, my 3D receive cube was empty. If somebody tried to reach me via a 3D hologram, his or her face would appear in it. At the same time, their recorded voice would tell me why they had contacted me. I told M4 about the problem.

"Adam, I've experienced the same problems in terms of trying to communicate with Soaa and Wo Ra since we left camp."

"M-Four, AF tried to repair my lenses while we searched for Dr. Browna. However, it failed. Can you fix them?"

"Hard to say. Airborne viruses keep shorting out their bio-circuits. A few minutes after I repaired bio-circuit H, J bio-circuit broke down. I fixed J and N bio-circuit shorted out."

My stomach muscles tightened. "We should spread out, then look for Soaa. When we find her, let's search for Dr. Browna."

"Affirmative."

To my right, Xa Om shoved flies off his wrist. "These insects never stop biting."

I looked up. "More volcanic dust is falling."

Xa Om glanced at the sky. "Not again."

Far away, a rumbling became louder.

"My MAW readings indicate that the volcano is erupting

again."

I cringed. "M-Four, does your MAW indicate that lava flows are headed this way?"

"There is a sixteen percent chance they are."

Soaa rushed out of the jungle.

"Soaa, where were you?" blurted Xa Om.

"Co-collecting mushrooms."

I told Soaa about our recent conversation with Hae Lana.

"Ah-amazing."

Wo Ra pointed to the sky. "Volcanic ash is falling."

My mind raced, trying to come up with a plan that would help us survive. "M-Four, can you carry Hae Lana? We must head for higher ground immediately."

"Affirmative. The area around the originator is the safest destination."

I nodded. "Let's go there."

M4 entered the dome Hae Lana was kept. Inside, a neck-mounted gravitational puller—NMGP—lifted Hae Lana off the bed. Within seconds, Hae Lana was floating behind my robot colleague's waist. M4 stepped out of the dome.

Hae Lana glowered. "I don't like facing backward."

"My NMGP is designed so that your body is aimed in that direction."

"That is true. Even so it irritates me."

I blinked, surprised. "M-Four, your NMGP didn't work before."

"Affirmative. I am amazed that it functions properly. Two of its bio-circuit boards updated themselves eight seconds ago. As a result my NMGP operates even though it's a proto-type that hasn't been field-tested yet."

"Everybody, let's go," I said.

After passing several groves, M4 said, "My MAW has been creating a field assistant robot—FAR—for the last two hours."

"Wow," commented Xa Om.

M4 removed a tiny disk from her arm, then placed it on a small bush. The bush expanded and changed into a six-foot-tall humanoid android with metallic green skin.

"I am FAR eleven," the machine said.

I paused, amazed. "FAR, can you protect us from beasts?"

"Without hesitation."

"It sounds like M-Four," said Wo Ra.

"M-Four, I can walk," remarked Hae Lana.

"As you wish." Hae Lana stood on her own, turned, and hiked.

To my right, Wo Ra said, "Wow, Hae Lana, you have recovered."

She glowered. "No shit."

Wo Ra blinked.

Hae Lana walked faster. "Adam, are you sure this is the best route?"

"Nearby pallas said that it is," replied Xa Om.

"Relying on a tree's comments strikes me as a bad idea. Is this the best we can do?"

My back muscles tensed up. "Yes."

"Adam, you put too much faith in Xa Om and Wo Ra's advice."

I bit my lip, irritated by her comment. "Their advice is sound."

"Are you sure?"

"Yes."

"You're naive. I could come up with a better plan."

"Assuming that you're right, what is it?"

She glared at me. "Judging by your tone, you don't believe me."

My stomach muscles tensed up. "Ignore my tone. What is your plan?"

"There is too much dense undergrowth in this spot. The

area to our right is easier to hike through."

"Hae Lana is correct," said FAR. "The area on our right is easier to hike through."

"A Bolra is in the area to our right," remarked Xa Om.

Hae Lana glanced in that direction. "I don't see it and my contact lenses don't detect any."

"Hae Lana is correct. There aren't any," FAR said.

"Several kapoks indicated that one is there. If we go around that spot, it will probably leave us alone," commented Wo Ra.

Hae Lana sighed. "How would you know that? You're just a child."

Wo Ra flinched.

Hae Lana shook her head. "Wo Ra, you are wrong. I know what I'm talking about."

"Hae Lana is correct," FAR said.

M4 looked at FAR. "Is your latest scan accurate?"

"It is."

I bit my lip, irritated. "Let's go to the right."

CHAPTER FORTY-FOUR

Our crew tramped between shiringas. On my left, M4 said, "This route is lighter, not as poorly illuminated as our prior course."

"That is true," I said.

Ahead a butterfly came to rest on a branch. Wo Ra pointed at it. "It is pretty."

"Yes it is," said Xa Om.

"Everybody should listen to me more often," bragged Hae Lana.

"Correct," agreed FAR.

"No shit. FAR is more alert than M-Four, and M-Four makes a lot of mistakes," snapped Hae Lana.

"I wouldn't put it that way," remarked Xa Om.

Hae Lana glared at him. "How would you put it?"

"Although M-Four isn't perfect, she notices a lot more than we do."

"Who is we?" blurted Hae Lana.

"You don't have to be nasty about it," commented Xa Om.

Hae Lana glowered. "I'm being realistic. Better get used to it."

Xa Om sighed. "By we I mean humans, Aito, and other humanoids."

"You put too much faith in M-Four. Her bio-circuits have been disrupted by viruses, streptococcus, and who knows what else."

"Have you examined her bio-circuits?" Xa Om asked.

"Why are you arguing with me?" snapped Hae Lana.

"He is pointing out that you need more facts," I said.

"I have all the facts that I need. Both of you should examine yours more closely."

"Hae Lana's comments are important," said FAR.

Hae Lana smirked. "Damn right."

My mind sped up, trying to come up with a solution that would help us get along. "We need to reach higher ground, not lapse into endless debate."

"If everybody took me more seriously, reaching higher ground would be easy."

Soaa shook her head.

Hae Lana frowned. "Soaa, why did you do that?"

"No-no reason."

Hae Lana scowled. "And your tone bothers me."

Soaa shrugged.

"Soaa wants us to survive," said Xa.

Hae Lana glowered. "So do I. Doesn't everybody see that? It doesn't look that way to me."

I thought of telling Hae Lana to be more reasonable. However, I didn't know if she would cooperate. Getting along with her was tough. Ahead, birds with leathery skin hopped from branch to branch.

M4 pointed at them. "Those species are unfamiliar. They resemble winged lizards."

"Who cares? They're harmless. M-Four, your endless chatter bores me," remarked Hae Lana.

I glared at her. "Let M-Four talk."

Hae Lana glowered. "Her remarks are a bunch of useless comments."

"They're helpful comments," said Xa Om.

Hae Lana glared at him. "Whose side are you on?"

"Nobodies' side."

"You're on her side, not mine and I don't like it."

"I am sorry that you don't."

"You don't sound sorry to me. I think you're lying."

"I said I was sorry. What else do you want?"

Hae Lana sneered. "Your respect. So far I've been patient, but everybody needs to be more polite when I talk."

"They are polite," Xa Om told her.

"They are not. They pretend to be. However, behind that facade, they think that I'm rude and don't know what I'm talking about. But I do know."

I paused as my back tensed up. "We need to walk in silence for a while. That way we can pay close attention to our surroundings."

Hae Lana glowered. "But . . ." She winced and mumbled incoherently.

Soon our group passed worms. On our right, a Bolra rushed out of vines, and gashed Xa Om's hip with its horn. Beams struck the creature. It bellowed. *Ommah.* Then it spun around, galloped behind dangling vines and disappeared, hidden by them.

Xa Om moaned. M4 sprayed the wound. "I can't walk."

"I'll carry you," said M4. She turned. Her NMGP lifted Xa Om and everybody resumed the journey.

Hae Lana glowered. "If everybody had been paying close attention, we could have shot that beast and scared it away before it attacked Xa Om."

Xa Om shook his head. "We were paying close attention."

Hae Lana scowled. "It's obvious that nobody was."

Above us, a humming grew louder. I glanced in that direction. A blue triangular spacecraft, about eighty feet long, seventy feet wide descended until it was about ninety feet above the trees. Much to my surprise, it stopped.

On my right, Hae Lana pointed up. "Why has it come here?"

To my left, M4 replied, "An important question."

"My lenses can't ID it," said Hae Lana.

"Mine can't either," said FAR in monotone.

"According to my MAW, it just sent a message," replied M4.

I blinked, caught off guard. "What does the message say?"

"Translating it will take time. It consists of high pitch whistling noises. So far, they are random."

Hae Lana sighed. "It's a bunch of meaningless sounds. Ignore it."

I bit my lip, irritated by Hae Lana's comment. "M-Four, try to translate it."

"Why do that? It's a waste of time," remarked Hae Lana.

My neck muscles tensed up. "It's possible that M-Four's MAW can detect order in the randomness."

"Fine. But don't blame me when her MAW discovers that I was right. It's only a bunch of pointless sounds."

I bit my lip, disappointed by Hae Lana's attitude. "I won't blame you."

"The spacecraft is getting bigger," Wo Ran called out.

"It's expanding sideways. Now it's larger than this entire grove," commented Xa Om.

CHAPTER FORTY-FIVE

Hae Lana stood away from the spacecraft. "Wow. It keeps expanding in every direction. I don't believe what I'm seeing. Is it going to shoot at us?"

"Shoot at us? Hard to say," replied M4.

"Hae Lana, you're too paranoid," said Xa Om.

"I'm pragmatic."

"Hae Lana is realistic," commented FAR.

The ship became transparent and vanished.

"Where did it go?" asked Xa Om.

"Th-that's what I was thinking," remarked Soaa.

"My MAW can't detect it," said M4.

I faced M4. "Has your MAW translated the message?"

"Not at this point."

"Good luck with that," Hae Lana said.

To our right, about eighty yards away, flames spread.

M4 pointed at the flames. "The jungle is on fire. It's coming this way."

I winced. "Let's retrace our steps, then take the other route."

M4 looked at Hae Lana. "Your suggestion to head in this direction was a bad plan."

"Stop giving me a hard time. Everybody makes mistakes."

"Your mistake was dangerous," said Xa Om.

"Back off. It was an honest decision."

The entire group spun around, then jogged. Behind us, a crackling grew louder.

"All of us need to move faster," I blurted.

Wo Ra glanced over her shoulder. "The fire keeps spread-ing."

CHAPTER FORTY-SIX

The entire group reached a safe area, then turned right and kept going. I sighed. "Keep up the pace. We need to reach higher ground ASAP."

M4 nodded. "Affirmative."

Hae Lana glared at M4.

M4 stared straight ahead, ignoring her.

"M-Four, you like taunting me," Hae Lana yelled.

"I do not."

"I'm getting used to your lies."

"I'm not lying."

Hae Lana scoffed, "Fine. However, you don't fool me with your cool, detached responses. I'm onto you."

M4 kept going, not responding.

Hae Lana glowered. "Robots are designed to be flawless. However, they don't know how to use intuition. As a result, they make more mistakes. I see it. Why others don't bother me."

FAR remained silent.

"Hae Lana, you complain a lot," said Wo Ra.

"Young lady, if you think more about my comments, you would realize that they are more accurate than just about anything that M-Four or others say."

"Hae Lana, Wo Ra is correct," remarked Soaa. "You do complain a lot."

Hae Lana glowered but didn't say anything.

To our right, a crackling became louder.

"Oh no," Hae Lana exclaimed.

"The fire is coming this way," said FAR.

Soaa looked over her shoulder at the flames. "Di-difficulty."

Our group slogged on.

To my left, M4 said, "Wo Ra, you're always trembling. What's wrong?"

"I am scared and I miss mom."

"I miss her, too," said Xa Om.

On my right, Soaa remarked, "According to lupunas, there is a Teog close by."

"I don't see it," replied Hae Lana. "You're wrong."

FAR nodded. "Hae Lana is correct. Soaa you are wrong."

"Ac-according to them, it's ahead of us, sixty yards away."

Hae Lana shook her head. "You and your ridiculous trees."

"My MAW has detected the beast. It's hiding behind strangler figs, coming this way," said M4.

"M-Four, knock it off. Your shitty information is useless."

"Hae Lana, pay attention to M-Four and Soaa's warnings," I said.

Hae Lana glared at me. "Yes sir."

"According to several wimba, it is on our left, hiding behind them," said Wo Ra.

My adrenaline pumped harder. "I can't see the beast and my lenses can't detect it."

"Its body odor asked the wimba to spray mist. They did. The mist confuses everybody's lenses," said M4.

"Mist can't confuse them," commented FAR.

"I agree with FAR," said Hae Lana.

"You said robots are flawed. Why do you trust FAR?" retorted Wo Ra.

Hae Lana glowered. "You're a child. Don't argue with me."

"Everybody, stay alert. If the Teog attacks fire at will," I said.

Hae Lana scoffed. "Shoot at something that isn't there. That is ridiculous."

Ahead, the creature rushed out of shadows, then darted behind a kapok. M4 and I fired. The beams struck dirt, missing the target.

"Adam, what were both of you shooting at?" exclaimed Hae Lana.

"The Teog."

"I didn't see it," remarked FAR.

Hae Lana glowered. "Of course you didn't. It wasn't there."

"It was," said M4.

Hae Lana sighed. "M-Four, Adam, both of you are too jumpy, seeing things that aren't there."

"I saw it," commented Wo Ra.

Hae Lana frowned. "If that is true, why didn't you shoot at it?"

"Hae Lana's question is an excellent one," said FAR.

"It moved too fast. It went behind the kapok before I could respond."

"Al although I didn't see it, the kapok's charges indicated that it was behind them," remarked Soaa.

"I didn't see it. However, I agree with Soaa," said Xa Om.

Hae Lana shook her head. "Like I said, just about everybody is too jumpy, seeing a creature that wasn't there."

My stomach muscles tightened. Ahead, the Teog darted out from behind a strangler fig.

"Look out," shouted Xa Om.

Chills raced up my spine. M4 and I fired. Our beams struck the creature. It screeched. *Yeeoot.* The predator sprinted toward us, its fangs bared.

As my adrenaline pumped faster, it slashed my right sleeve. I dodged to the left, blasting. *Yeeeot.* It clawed M4's neck. She ducked, spraying ammo. *Yeeoot.*

The predator reached down and swiped her chest. Beams

from our weapons struck its neck and ear. *Yeeeot.* It turned right, sprinted past Wo Ra, then raced into the jungle and vanished, hidden by gigantic leaves.

Xa Om rushed to M4. "Are your hurt?"

"No."

"The wounds are deep."

They vanished.

Xa Om flinched. "You heal fast. I've never seen that before."

"My internal nano robots are designed that way."

I looked over at Wo Ra. "Are you hurt?"

"No. I scraped my leg. It is not serious."

M4 examined Wo Ra's leg. "It could get infected." She sprayed it with her knuckle-mounted nozzle.

Wo Ra sighed.

"You're still trembling," noted M4.

"I-I a-am, I am . . ."

"Scared. I can tell. You don't have to explain," remarked M4.

The girl exhaled.

"Breathing out slowly is a good way to release tension. By the way, I figured out how to get rid of the Teog."

I blinked, surprised. "How?"

"The noise we make as our group hikes creates temporary turbulent shapes in the air. The Teog use them as a guide to locate us. However, sometimes, those shapes vanish because sounds made by worms or insects break them apart."

I paused, curious.

"If the sounds aren't loud enough, the Teog use strange attractors, shapes our body odor creates, to follow us. Knowing this, I programmed my MAW to send fake attractor body odors, ones that are identical to ours, to another part of the jungle. From this point on, if the Teog come close to our group, they will end up searching for us in another location."

"Great," I said. "I assume the fake attractor body odors didn't include yours. Is that correct?"

"That is correct."

"Judging by that blank look on your face, M-Four, I feel like you are not impressed by your ac-accomplishment," said Wo Ra.

"I'm designed to help Adam and his crew. It's my job. I don't know anything about joy, pride, anger, hate or the other emotions."

Wo Ra gasped. "Emotions are important."

M4 had a blank look in her eyes.

"Let's keep going," I said.

CHAPTER FORTY-SEVEN

Soon our group walked between dimly lit lilies, all of them partly obscured by mist.

Hae Lana sighed. "This part of the Glorm is threatening. It feels as if we've traveled back to prehistoric times."

Xa Om nodded. "I agree. This area gives me the willies. It's early afternoon, yet it's so dark that it looks like night."

On our left, a line of four-inch beetles with huge claws marched over leaves.

Xa Om pointed at the insects. "They smell like rotten flesh."

Wo Ra vomited, then spoke in a hoarse voice, "The odor upset my stomach."

Ahead, a few six-inch frogs with three eyes, croaked. Not far beyond them, a five-inch-long mosquito touched down on a flytrap.

Hae Lana pointed at the insect. "That mosquito has feces in its mouth. It's eating it. Disgusting."

"The mosquito keeps the Glorm clean," M4 said.

Hae Lana shook her head. "It is disgusting. Only you would think it's interesting, M-Four."

M4 ignored her. "We should reach a higher elevation soon. At that point, our group will have a better chance of avoiding any more lava flows and fires."

"Glad to hear it," I said.

At dusk, our group set up camp. On our shoulder pads, lights switched on.

"I'll have to sleep in my clothes," Xa Om said. "My dome won't open. M-Four, why won't it?"

"According to eighteen graphs, mutated staphylococcus and viruses have shorted out its bio-logic boards."

Hae Lana scowled. "My dome won't open either. Great, fucking great. Any insect can bite us whenever they want."

I turned to M4. "Can the dome's bio-logic boards repair themselves?"

"According a computer model, there is a nineteen percent chance that they will."

Hae Lana winced. "Assuming they do, when will that happen?"

"There are three estimated times. In an hour and nine minutes. Twenty-one hours from now or thirty-two hours from now."

"Three estimated times? M-Four did you make that up? It sounds stupid."

"I did not make it up. All three times are based on quantum mechanics modeling. That modeling, like quantum mechanics, takes the most energy efficient route to come up accurate answers."

Hae Lana glowered. "It sounds like a bunch of bat shit to me."

"It is not."

"Are you mocking me?"

"No. I am answering your question."

Hae Lana frowned. "It sounds like you are mocking me."

I placed a hand on Hae Lana's shoulder. "You need to calm down."

"I am. You need to relax."

Far away, somewhere in the dark, a clicking grew louder.

Hae Lana looked around. "What's making that noise? It's getting on my nerves."

"According to a lupuna, three flesh eating Tebos have

attacked each other," remarked Wo Ra.

"What is a Tebo?"

"It's similar to a spider. However, a Tebo can fly," replied Xa Om.

Hae Lana frowned. "How would you know it's similar to a spider?"

"There were ma-millions of Tebos on Yerak. All of them make a noise that is similar to the one we just heard."

Hae Lana winced. "I'm sorry I asked."

Everything vanished and was replaced by a jungle. On my right, M4 and Wo Ra took a few steps.

"How did we end up here?" asked Wo Ra.

"Good question," I replied.

"I don't see the others," said M4.

Chills went up my spine. "I don't see them either. M-Four, do you know what happened to them?"

"Not at this point. My MAW is evaluating our surroundings."

Ahead, a six-foot-long beetle crawled out of the shadows. I cringed. "Let's get out of here."

M4 nodded. "Excellent suggestion."

Our small group veered to the left, then passed towering weeds.

"All the plants are huge," commented M4.

Wo Ra nodded. "They sure are."

"Wo Ra, do you recognize their sounds?" M4 asked.

"No. They are different. The kapoks and other trees on Yerak's sounds were a steady stream of short and long beeps."

"Like Morse code."

Wo Ra paused. "What is that?"

"I'll explain when we're in a safer area."

Everybody reached the top of a hill and hiked over it.

To my left, an eight-foot-long ant crept out from behind a

gigantic blade of grass. My adrenaline pumped faster. I pointed in the opposite direction. "Let's go this way."

"This is frightening," said Wo Ra.

I glanced in her direction. "Yes."

Everything faded and was replaced by another jungle.

"Another fast change. This is awful," said Wo Ra.

I flinched. "Yes."

"Constant, unexpected change can be demanding," remarked M4.

I looked at Wo Ra. "You're trembling."

"I am."

"Under these circumstances trembling is a natural response," M4 said.

Wo Ra examined the plants around us closer. "I recognize these kapoks and the adjacent strangler figs. We're a short distance from my village."

"Interesting," said M4.

I blinked, taken aback. "Wo Ra, which route should we take?"

She pointed to the right. "This way."

"Where are the Kicra?"

"They're on our left, about two miles away."

I exhaled.

Our small group entered the village, then stopped near a hut. Ze Ma and Xa Om stepped out of it.

Wo Ra ran to them. "Father, mother, it's good to see you."

Ze Ma's mouth tightened. "I'm not your mother."

"But you are. Don't you recognize me?" blurted Wo Ra.

Xa Om flinched. "No. This is a cruel hoax."

"You don't recognize your own daughter?" exclaimed Wo Ra.

Ze Ma recoiled. "She died three years ago. And she didn't look like you."

"Go away. Stop taunting us," said Xa Om.

Wo Ra started trembling.

I touched her shoulder. "Let's go."

M4 faced the strangers "Sorry to offend. There are has been a misunderstanding."

Xa Om flinched. "You are aliens with strange ways."

Our small group turned and departed. Without warning, everything became fuzzy, broke apart and was replaced by a spot in the Glorm.

In the near distance, Hae Lana frowned. "M-Four, Adam and Wo Ra, all three of you disappeared a few minutes ago. Why?"

My mind raced, trying to come up with an answer.

Hae Lana scowled. "Your disappearance doesn't make sense. However, there has to be a reasonable explanation for it."

"At this point, coming up with a reasonable explanation is difficult," said M4.

Behind Hae Lana, Xa Om said, "Did all three of you go someplace else after you vanished?"

M4 answered.

Xa Om paused. "Fascinating."

"My lenses aren't offering any answers regarding your disappearance," snapped Hae Lana. "It bothers me that my lenses aren't. IT should have designed better ones. Their sloppy work shows me how foolish they are."

"They can't evaluate every situation," I said.

Hae Lana glowered. "That's their job."

Xa Om glanced at Hae Lana. "You have to be patient."

"I am. IT screwed up. As a result, I have to put up with their mistakes."

FAR nodded. "Hae Lana is correct. They did screw it up."

Wo Ra trembled.

M4 stood beside her. "You are scared."

She nodded.

"If I can soothe your nerves, let me know."

"I appreciate it."

"Wo Ra, Soaa and Xa Om, your English has improved one hundred percent. Nanites in your lenses have improved your ability to learn faster," M4 said.

"Although I don't know what nanites are, thank you," Xa Om answered.

Soaa tilted her head. "How-how do the nanites do this?"

"They alter your DNA with genetic scissors. As a result, your hippocampus retains more information," explained M4.

Wo Ra rubbed her face. "M-Four, your explanation is full of new words, ones that are difficult for me to understand."

Hae Lana scowled. "Adam, you're in charge. You should have planned our goals better."

Adam is doing his best," said M4.

Hae Lana pointed at her. "I'm not talking to you."

M4 had a blank expression on her face.

"We must reach higher ground," I said.

"Affirmative," said M4.

Soon Hae Lana vanished. I flinched. "Where did she go?"

"Intriguing question," said M4.

Xa Om paused, his brow tight in concentration.

I turned to Xa Om. "Have any of the surrounding lupunas or other trees mentioned the reason for her disappearance?"

"No. Two of them say it's an occurrence that baffles them."

"I-I agree with Xa Om," remarked Soaa.

M4 turned to Wo Ra. "Have the adjacent kapoks mentioned this topic?"

She flinched. "They say somebody is communicating with her."

I faced Wo Ra. "Who is somebody? It's a vague statement."

Wo Ra paused, trembling. "I don't know."

"I-I don't know either," said Soaa.

"Don't slow down. If we do lava may sweep us away," I said.

Everybody trudged on.

After passing three groves, Hae Lana appeared on my right. I blinked, surprised. "What happened to you?"

CHAPTER FORTY-EIGHT

She winced. "A second after leaving this place I ended up in a desert. About two hundred yards away, five ten-foot-tall tan reptiles with long snouts were rushing in my direction. As my adrenaline pumped, they stopped about twelve feet from me. Then they hissed and started circling me."

My body went cold.

Hae Lana flinched. "When two were on my left, they growled. Within seconds, they along with the desert faded and I ended up here."

Xa Om's jaw muscles tightened.

Hae Lana frowned. "Nobody believes me, though it's true. I saw it."

"Ne-nearby kapoks don't know what to say about it," remarked Soaa.

Hae Lana clenched her teeth. "Soaa, you don't believe me."

"It-it could be true. However, adjacent strangler figs indicate that you stopped making noise. That was their only comment."

"For the sake of argument, let's say it's true. If so, why did it happen?" remarked M4.

Hae Lana sighed. "I don't have a clue."

"Did your lenses photograph the desert or scan it?" I asked.

"For unknown reasons, they didn't. That frustrates me."

"Let's keep going. We have to reach higher ground," I said.

"This is high enough," Hae Lana snapped.

"Hae Lana is correct," agreed FAR.

I bit my lip, irritated by her comment. "No it isn't."

Hae Lana glared at me. Our group kept going.

Within minutes, we came upon another hill, one that was the same height as the others. Ahead, to our right, lava flowed down a gully.

I pointed at it, "Watch out."

"I see it. Do you think I'm blind?" blurted Hae Lana.

My neck muscles tensed up.

"We're surrounded by lava. There is no escape," said M4.

"Time to die," Hae Lana called out. "Adam, you should have planned better."

I winced. Everything turned grey and was replaced by a beach.

"We've been transported to another spot. How did that happen?" pondered FAR.

On my right, Hae Lana glowered. "It doesn't make sense."

To my left, weeds on a dune shook, blown by the wind.

I blinked, amazed. Above the dune, clouds moved over two star-like suns. "M-Four, are we on Isal?"

"Not at this point."

"That's impossible," exclaimed Hae Lana. "It violates the laws of physics. There must be a common-sense explanation for this change."

M4 looked at her. "If you know one, I want to hear it. This sudden change violates everything I know. On the other hand, here we are."

Further down the beach, a tiny figure raced toward us.

I flinched. "Who is that? My lenses' MCIT has broken down."

Hae Lana fiddled with hers. "Mine isn't working either. Damn it"

"It's Dr. Browna," said M4.

"It can't be. She died," exclaimed Hae Lana.

CHAPTER FORTY-NINE

Browna stopped in front of us, panting. "All of you are here. How did that happen?"

M4 answered her.

"Dr. Browna, you're alive. It's astonishing," commented Xa Om.

"It's more than astonishing," remarked Hae Lana.

I mentioned our search for her. "Dr. Browna, what happened to you?"

She blinked. "One minute I was in the Glorm. The next thing I knew I was in a trench filled with mud. I heard distant artillery firing. On my right, a soldier in an unfamiliar uniform rushed toward me. He told me they needed a medic and ordered me to go with him. I didn't know how this stranger recognized me but I didn't know who he was. It might have been my yellow armband."

"Who cares," snapped Hae Lana.

I glared at her. "Dr. Browna, keep going."

"He told me to quit stalling and follow him. I did. Within seconds, we reached a soldier who was on his back. The soldier screamed. Blood was coming out of the bottom of his ear. The top half had been blown off. I reached inside a chest pocket, grabbed a syringe, and injected Vot into a nearby area to numb the pain. Then the bleeding stopped. I cleaned the wound and wrapped the ear in bandages."

"It sounds like you were a medic," commented M4.

Browna flinched. "Yes. I read about them years ago. Their equipment was primitive."

Hae Lana blurted, "This is freakish, hard to believe."

Browna glowered. "I can hardly believe it myself."

I said, "Keep going."

Browna sighed. "At any rate, after treating this soldier, another told me that three more needed help. He led me to them. One's finger was blown off. I was closing the wound when a screeching noise came from behind me. A soldier yelled that something was approaching. My guess was that a mortar shell was headed our way. It struck a nearby spot. Much to my surprise, everything vanished and I ended up on this beach. That was two mornings ago."

Hae Lana glowered. "Did you make any of this up?"

Browna frowned. "Absolutely not."

Hae Lana shook her head. "It can't be true."

Browna glowered. "Why?"

Hae Lana bit her lip. "It just can't be. There must be another explanation."

I blinked, surprised by these events. "M-Four, do you have an explanation?"

"According to five computer models, an alien race has transported us here and the other locations because it wants us to survive."

Hae Lana shook her head. "Alien race? I don't think so."

"Why did this race send us to so many different places?" I asked M4.

"According to all my probes this race of beings can't recognize our DNA because they have never encountered anything like it before."

Browna glowered. "An alien race doesn't recognize our DNA. How can that be?"

"According to a holographic model, one possibility is that the race is a machine, a device that has forgotten what a sentient being is," replied M4.

Hae Lana scoffed. "A machine that is forgotten was a

sentient being is? Oh come on. That can't be true."

I gave Hae Lana a stern look. "Let M-Four finish."

"Probability charts indicate that the process might have taken billions of years for the machine to forget what a sentient being is," said M4.

"What is the other possibility?" asked Browna.

"This race has evolved, become a planet or a jungle, life forms that don't recognize our DNA."

Hae Lana paused. "Unreal."

Browna frowned. "Does the computer model offer any proof?"

"No, only educated guesses. Their DNA evolved, updated itself in order to survive. It's possible that the only way this race could have survived is by taking on another life form or forms," said M4.

Hae Lana groaned. "Ridiculous."

"Is there another possibility, M-Four?" asked Browna.

"This race isn't flora or fauna. It's something else. It might be similar to the quantum. As a result, it doesn't know if we're plants or animals so it's hard to figure out where we would survive. For want of a better term, I'll use the term Newa for race. At any rate, the Newa sent us to several planets or moons, locations in different universes. When we're on the verge of dying, the Newa transported us to another planet or moon because they realized what our limitations are."

I blinked. "Amazing."

Hae Lana sighed. "This is speculation. It might be wrong."

"Wrong? Speculation? Both could be true," admitted M4.

Browna glowered. "Hae Lana, do you have a more accurate explanation?"

"Quit giving me a hard time."

"I'm not giving you a hard time. I want the truth. In other words, give me a more accurate explanation."

"I don't have any yet. However, coming up with a better

one could be easy. It just takes a little more time."

I ignored them. "Most forms of life are based on carbon. What about the Newa?"

"At some point in the distant past they were," explained M4. "However, according to another quantum computer model, they created smart robots. The robots improved themselves morning, noon, and night, nonstop. The next generation of robots altered the Newa's DNA. As a result, the Newa evolved to the point where their DNA included carbon, silicon and other elements. As a result, the Newa could evolve into other life forms."

I blinked, surprised. "What kind of life forms?"

"Unlike the former possibility, this one was more complex. However, the end result was that Newa were transformed into jungles, moons, planets, oceans, stars."

"That sort of evolution is impossible," retorted Hae Lana.

"It does sound far-fetched," commented Browna.

"Dr. Browna, how do you explain our recent experiences?" asked M4.

"Hmmm. I'll have to think about it."

Hae Lana frowned. "There has to be a reasonable explanation. Turning into jungles, moons, planets, and stars is ridiculous."

M4 turned to Hae Lana. "If you have a reasonable explanation please tell me what it is."

"You're being a smartass."

"M-Four, are you telling me that jungles, moons, planets and stars are intelligent and can solve problems?" I asked.

"Affirmative."

"How do they do it?" asked Browna.

"Kapoks ca-can communicate with each other. As a result, they solve problems," commented Xa Om.

M4's turned to him. "Xa Om, exactly. Here is another explanation. Viruses and bacteria spread through the jungle and start killing kapoks, strangler figs, and other trees. A few trees change their bark or their leaves. As a result, they survive. Then they share that information with other trees and more survive."

Hae Lana sighed. "Maybe."

Wo Ra smiled. "Kapoks are smart."

M4 nodded. "Affirmative."

"Can moons solve problems?" I asked.

"Some can. Others, not so much," said M4.

"Why some and not others?"

"If a moon is too close to a star it's surface becomes so hot that all water on its surface boils away. As a result, it's harder for bacteria, a form of life to survive."

"That sounds realistic," said Hae Lana.

M4 explained further. "However, if the Newa created that star, it's possible that it can reduce its surface temperature. As a result, bacteria on a nearby moon thrives. Eventually, the bacteria evolve and create jungles. Millions of years later, a race of sentient beings along with intelligent jungles create smarter sentient life based on carbon, silicon, and other elements."

Hae Lana frowned. "That is wild speculation."

"It may answer the question regarding how we got here," said Browna.

"Why would they use silicon along with other elements?" I asked M4. "Carbon-based life is the norm."

"Silicon along with other graphene and other elements makes it easier for them to thrive, not die, on many other moons and planets."

Hae Lana glowered. "That is unrealistic."

"According to the computer model, the Newa have thrived."

I persisted with my queries. "Can the Newa create stars? Any technology that can do it is so sophisticated that it boggles my mind."

"Create stars? Ridiculous. They aren't smart enough to do that," blurted Hae Lana.

"According to the model, they can," said M4.

Hae Lana shook her head. "Show me."

A 3D hologram appeared in front of M4. In it a star pulsated. She pointed at the star. "This is Lonto. The Newa created this four million six thousand years ago."

Browna gazed at the 3D hologram of Lonto. "Spectacular."

M4 nodded. "Affirmative."

Hae Lana paused, her brow contorted in concentration.

"What technique did the Newa use to create this celestial body?" I asked.

"Backpropagation in neural networks. In other words, the Newa learn by their mistakes," M4 answered.

Hae Lana frowned. "That would take billions of years."

M4 looked at her. "Perhaps. They use trillions of bio-machines, devices that are similar to quantum computers and the brain. The machines update themselves every few minutes. As a result, they solve problems faster."

"Fascinating," said Browna.

I agreed with Browna. "Are you saying that a moon, a planet, and a star that Newa created are bio-machines?"

M4 nodded. "For want of a better term, yes. However, their bio-machines evolve trillions of times faster than ordinary stars, moons, and planets."

Hae Lana flinched. "Astounding."

"The bio-machines also used and use quantum entanglement to share information. That information makes it possible for them to learn faster because they are aware of more mistakes."

"Did the Newa send us here?" I asked M4.

"According to another computer model, they used the originator to do that."

Soaa's brow tight in concentration.

"The originator did that. Nice," said Wo Ra.

Xa Om nodded. "Yes, nice."

FAR opened its mouth but didn't say anything.

Browna blinked. "Spectacular. Do you know anything about Isal's gravity being out of phase?"

"Affirmative," said M4. "The gravitational pull changed, was out of phase at specific intervals, because the planet itself was altering its surface. That alteration included and includes its jungles, mountains, deserts, rivers, streams, lakes and oceans."

Browna's eyes opened wider. "Did the Newa initiate DNA improvement, quicker neural adaptation, and better quantum tunneling in cells, processes in all the flora and fauna on the planets and moons they created?"

"According to a computer model, affirmative."

Browna's jaw dropped. "Would all these processes make it possible for all the fauna on these planets and moons to live longer because their cells could and did destroy cancer cells, deadly phage, and lethal viruses?"

"Affirmative."

"Did the Newa create those buildings on Yerak?" I asked.

"According to my database, they did," replied M4.

"Did the Newa create the humanoids that Doland saw?"

"Affirmative."

Browna interrupted my questioning. "Why did they create them?"

"The Newa were testing the crew, wanted to study their reactions to unrecognizable entities," answered M4.

"Did the Newa create the sculpture?" I asked, before Browna could ask another question.

"Affirmative," answered M4.

Browna's forehead tightened in concentration. "Did they create them to test the crew's reactions?"

M4 nodded. "Affirmative."

"Were the sculptures the Newa themselves?" I asked M4.

"They were Newa cavemen."

I blinked, surprised. "What else was on the surface of the originators?"

"Smart leptons."

"What are those?"

"Ninety percent of the time, leptons, common place subatomic particles interact with protons and other subatomic particles randomly. However, smart leptons, ones created by the Newa, interact with other subatomic particles sixty billion times faster, not randomly. As a result, the Newa themselves along with the plants and animals they created evolve faster. As a result, this race of beings and the flora and the fauna they created are eighty-four percent more likely to survive."

The End

ABOUT THE AUTHOR

December 2019, I moved to Orinda, California. I'm retired, used to work in market research. When I'm not writing science fiction, I draw or paint pictures.

My website-> thadde.net/w/wr.html